Loveswept ® 874

MS. MILLER
AND THE
MIDAS MAN

MARY KAY
McCOMAS

DNEY · AUCKLAND

MS. MILLER AND THE MIDAS MAN

A Bantam Book / February 1998

ISBN 0-553-44616-9

Published simultaneously in the United States and Canada

Bantam Books are published by Bantam Books, a division of Bantam Dou-
bleday Dell Publishing Group, Inc. Its trademark, consisting of the words
"Bantam Books" and the portrayal of a rooster, is Registered in U.S.
Patent and Trademark Office and in other countries. Marca Registrada.
Bantam Books, 1540 Broadway, New York, New York 10036.

PRINTED IN THE UNITED STATES OF AMERICA

OPM   0 9 8 7 6 5 4 3 2 1

This one is for Sue Noyes.
Thanks for the cool Web page.

ONE

The whole town was atwitter with the news.

Scott Hammond was back and nothing would be dull or boring again—according to the gossip. This very same, totally reliable source of information also claimed he could leap tall buildings in a single bound, snatch small children from the paths of speeding locomotives, and resurrect truth, justice, and the American Way within the local school system with one hand tied behind his back.

Augusta Miller was no skeptic. She wanted to believe in magic and fairy tales as much as the next person. Truly. But experience had taught her that fairy tales just weren't true, and unfortunately, *the next person* didn't have Scott Hammond for a next-door neighbor.

"Lydia, he's back," she whispered loudly over the phone.

"Who?"

"You *know* who. From next door. He's back. It's the third time this week. Can I call the police now?"

"No," her sister said, her voice tight with strained patience. "That's not the way things are handled in small towns. What's he doing?"

"Same as before," she said, leaning over the kitchen sink to stare back at the intruder. "Sitting in the middle of my backyard with his garbage strewn all over. Staring. Drooling."

"Can't you just ignore him? He'll get bored and go home eventually."

"And leave his trash behind," she added, spotting a stray bread crumb on the counter, brushing it into the palm of her hand, and tossing it into the trash. "If he steps in my new flower beds, I'll shoot him. I swear. I'm not at all happy with this new neighbor of mine."

"Well, try talking to him."

"Who?"

"You *know* who. In your backyard. Talk to him nicely and maybe he'll move back to his own yard."

"Maybe I should use a little broomstick logic, huh?" she said, peering out at her uninvited guest once more. He was very big. He could probably snap a broomstick in half with his teeth.

"That's allowed. I don't think it would upset anyone if you shooed him away with a broom."

"What if he comes at me? Attacks me?"

"Well, then it would be okay to call the police, I'm sure."

Her sister's voice had taken on a great deal of humor that she didn't appreciate. "You've been a big help, Liddy. Thanks."

"Gus, honey, you're my favorite sister . . ."

"I'm your only sister."

"But you have to learn to lighten up a little. You're so like Mother sometimes, it scares me."

"Oh, now . . ."

"This isn't the big city. We're more tolerant of our neighbors here."

"Yes, well, there's tolerance and then there's being a gutless schmo who lets other people move in next door and take over."

"Attagirl, Gus. You march on out there and tell him what's what."

"I'm going to," she said, stretching the telephone cord to the broom closet. "And I'm taking my broom. Just in case."

She had a mental picture of Robin Hood fighting the sheriff off with a toothpick, but it was the best weapon she had.

"Good girl. Call me when the dust settles."

She hung up the phone and carried the broom to the back door, holding the calico curtains aside to check on the interloper. There he sat, staring and slobbering, the most enormous, gigantic dog she'd ever seen in her life. She swallowed around the lump of fear in her throat and turned the doorknob, making no sound at all, then jumped when he turned his large head in her direction.

"Look," she said, pushing the screen door open and taking one step out of the house. "I don't want to make you mad, but you and I are going to have to come to an understanding if we're going to be neighbors."

He continued to stare at her.

"Okay. First off, this is my yard. You live next door. I don't know how you keep getting the gate open, but you're not to do it anymore. Understand? You stay in your own yard and . . . and take your trash with you. Please."

Bertrum T. Goodfellow, Bert to his friends, was a reasonable animal. He didn't understand the woman's fear, but through the open gate he saw a barbecue-flavored Dog-Gone Dog Yummy land in the tall grass of *his habitat*. . . . And he did understand that.

Her heart raced with fear as she stood statue-still and watched in utter astonishment as the beast stood, shook himself from head to tail, ambled across her lawn, and moseyed through the garden gate as if he'd understood her completely and found her request to be reasonable.

Stunned by the simplicity of it, it was several more seconds before she hurried over to the tall gate to shut it and wedge a rock against the bottom, the latch being on the other side.

"All right," she said, most satisfied with herself. It had been some time, a long time, since she'd felt as if she had any control of her life. She wasn't exactly sure how she'd managed this small feat, but she wasn't above taking credit for it. She was pleased.

And angry when she turned around and saw the trash scattered across her tiny backyard.

"Okay. This is it. I've had it," she said to her neighbor's fence, tossing a beer can over the top. "I don't care who you are. I'm sick and tired of cleaning up your trash. And I'm sick and tired of finding it in my yard."

The fence had a dull despondent expression to it, its white paint peeling and chipped. It was an unsatisfactory target for the empty potato chip bag and the next two beer cans.

"The next time this happens, I'm calling—" she stopped, long-necked beer bottle poised mid-throw.

Would the police arrest a local hero for allowing his dog to trash her backyard? No, they'd just give him a stern talking to—if that. She sniffed indignantly. Maybe a hit man? She liked nipping problems in the bud.

"I'm calling . . . somebody. Somebody who'll tell you what's what and where to put your trash."

Technically, she should have a little talk with this new neighbor herself, she supposed. But sustaining a good head of anger for the time it would take to walk all the way to the front of the house, across the two driveways, onto his porch, and through an entire harangue simply wasn't in her lately. It was easier to throw the trash back over the fence.

Besides, she'd seen her new neighbor—tall, handsome, walked with long, sure strides. She wasn't what her sister, Lydia, called a worldly woman. Nor, in her opinion, was she particularly shy. Inexperienced described her better, and while scolding a tall, handsome man about his trash didn't seem beyond her, she imagined it would be rather . . . difficult, and preferred to avoid it.

Still, she was past being nice about it.

"I haven't said a word about the loud music. Very tolerant, I think. And I didn't mind that your friend parked his car in my driveway the other night. I wasn't going anywhere, anyway." She picked up a rotting banana peel with two fingers and flipped it over the fence. "But this is where I draw the line. Trash your own yard if you must. Don't mow it. Don't trim the bushes. Don't paint this pathetic fence." Another bottle and one more soda can went sailing. "I don't care if I have to live next door to the messiest house on the street. I don't. That's your business. But this yard is mine."

She turned with her hands on her hips and surveyed the small, neatly trimmed patch of grass outlined with rows of primrose, red coralbells, and lupines and the big elm tree that shaded it all with deep satisfaction. It wasn't big, but it was beautiful. And it was all hers.

On the other side of the rather forlorn looking fence, Scotty smiled and patiently counted the cans, bottles, and wrappers. Sixteen. Same as yesterday. Same as the day before. The banana peel, of course, had been Bert's idea—but he'd come home willingly for a single yummy, so he wouldn't reprimand the animal this time. Now, if the pattern held, his pretty neighbor was about to disappear inside her house again.

Her soliloquy was unexpected and amusing, and

he wasn't at all disappointed by the clear, even tone of her voice. It was a good sign that she was feeling chatty. Perhaps it was time to make his move. . . .

Slowly, so as not to make any noise, he unfolded his tall body from the lawn chair he'd parked himself in after tossing those few choice pieces of trash over the fence earlier. He left his copy of *A Midsummer Night's Dream* on the seat, tiptoed over a low bush and a hardy crop of garden weeds to the fence, and peered over.

She was the prettiest woman he'd ever seen. Not knock-'em-out beautiful like some, but pretty in a way that was hard to describe. Healthy. Wholesome. Sweet. All appropriate words, but not nearly enough to depict that quality about her that was also feminine and sexual in an earthy, lusty sort of way. She was a special, unique combination of woman, he thought, watching her stoop down to pinch dead-heads out of her flower garden.

It looked like her, the garden. Bright, neat, picture-book perfect. Maybe a little too perfect. A tiny bit of male . . . dishevelment wouldn't hurt—her or her garden. He'd been trying to catch her eye and start a conversation for some time now, but she either wouldn't look his way or would merely smile a little, avert her eyes, and walk quickly into her house.

She was wearing a long-sleeved springy looking dress, her dark hair was tied back at the nape of her neck, and she was barefoot, he noticed, making her seem as vulnerable and natural as he'd imagined her to be.

"There, you see, that nasty beast and his trash almost made me forget why I wanted to come out here in the first place," Gus told the foliage. "You need water, don't you?"

Scotty cleared his throat, loudly, and when she spun around to face him, he calmly looked about the yard before asking, "Were you . . . speaking to me?"

"What? No . . . Well, yes. Before. I was. But no," she stammered, getting to her feet.

"Did you throw all this trash into my backyard?"

"No. Well, yes. I did. But . . . it's not mine."

"It's not yours? What, it's borrowed? Stolen?"

"No. Of course not. It's . . . it's your trash," she said finally, too stunned at being caught talking to herself to think straight. Too mortified at being caught tossing trash, even if it *was* his, to speak coherently. And too overwhelmed by her disorderly neighbor's dazzling smile and friendly dark eyes to do much more than keep her knees from buckling under her.

"Are you sure?" he asked, enjoying himself, enjoying the stir of desire he'd come to expect whenever he saw her.

"What?"

"Are you sure it's my trash? It doesn't look familiar." He turned his head and winked at Bert.

The hundred-pound rottweiler yawned and appeared bored. Go next door. Come back. Human mating rituals were slow and tedious. He preferred a more obvious approach.

She frowned. She glanced at the back of Mrs. Falconetti's house, on the other side of hers. It was newly whitewashed, the shutters painted turquoise last fall, window boxes bulging with impatiens. . . . Her eyes slid back to the man.

" 'Course, it all looks pretty much the same, doesn't it?" he went on, grinning as he turned back to her. Killer dimples winked at her from both cheeks. "I guess I don't mind if you throw it over the fence, a little more isn't going to make much difference at this point. Just be careful when I'm sitting out here, okay?"

"I didn't know you were sitting there," she said, feeling foolish despite the fact that she had no reason to. "And I threw it in your yard because it belongs to you. Your animal brought it over here."

He gave her a dubious look to keep the fun going. "Well, if you say so, but . . ." Again he turned to Bert, who had sprawled out on his belly in the shade, completely aware that his job had been well done. "Bert," he said, reaching in his pocket for another barbecue-flavored Dog-Gone Dog Yummy. "Have you been in the garbage again?"

The dog wagged his tail and barked once for his reward.

"He's such a dog," he said, shaking his head as he turned back to her.

"Yes, he is," she said, mustering her resolve. "And I'd appreciate it if you'd keep him and your trash in your own yard."

"Okay," he said simply, leaning on the fence. All

he had to do was keep the gate latched. "Nice day, don't you think?"

"Yes. Very nice." Very like the last two weeks of fine summer weather. But warmer. Much, much warmer, now that she thought of it.

"When was the last time you saw a sky that blue?" he asked.

The day before, but for politeness' sake she looked at it again, then back at her neighbor. She could hardly take her eyes off him, as a matter of fact. He was tall—extremely tall, as the fence was high—with dark brown hair, his shoulders wide and thick under a cotton shirt, his bearing confident and easy. It was his eyes, however, that kept drawing her back to his face. Deep and dark like an all-consuming abyss. They were eyes a person could get lost in, disappear into. . . .

"Reminds me of when I was a kid," he said, flashing that smile again. "Bright blue sky. Long summer days with nothing to do."

She'd grown up in Seattle, where the sky was generally overcast. And if he had nothing to do, there was always his lawn and the fence and the trash and . . . She merely nodded and started toward the back door. She could water the flowers later.

"You didn't grow up here in Tylerville, did you?" he asked. He would have remembered her for sure. You didn't see eyes like hers every day. Clear and perceptive. Hazel green, was his guess from a distance. Wide open, they were, but they revealed little of what she was thinking.

"No."

"Where are you from?"

"Seattle originally. Then New York." She wasn't accustomed to telling strangers her life's story. But if they were going to be neighbors, and if she wished to keep *his* animal and *his* trash out of *her* yard, diplomatic relations were in order.

"And now Tylerville?" He chuckled. "You hiding from someone?"

"What?" She looked startled.

"No one moves to Tylerville, Indiana, without a good reason. Rural living is fashionable now, but . . . Tylerville? It's not exactly on the list of the ten best small towns to live in."

"Well, I like it." She didn't want to get into this with him. She had her reasons for moving to Tylerville, none of which concerned him. Besides, hadn't he just moved *back* to Tylerville? On purpose?

He made her nervous in a strange sort of way, as if he were interrogating her. He was watching her as if he'd like to crawl into her skin and make it his own, to know her that well.

"I grew up here," he said. And when she didn't seem particularly impressed by this, he added, "In this very house. My parents passed away a few years ago. I thought I'd come back and fix the place up."

This was when she might have asked where he'd been, what he'd been doing, why he hadn't come back sooner, if he planned to paint the house and the fence, if he'd had a happy childhood, or just about any other question she might come up with. But she didn't.

"I'm sorry about your parents."

Had she known them? Had she heard of the Hammond family? Was she from a large family? Was there going to be any additional information about *her* forthcoming? She was pretty tight-lipped for a woman, he thought. And in his mind, that was not a derogatory remark against her sex. It was simply one of the things he knew about women.

You see, if Scotty knew *anything*, he knew women. Nearly as many sisters as it would take to make a female basketball team, an ex-wife, a daughter, and several dozen female friends along the way made him an expert.

"They were pretty old," he said of his parents, as if that somehow made their passing easier. Truth to tell, he was already heading down another avenue of interest. "You've done a nice job on this old place. I like the flowers. Old Mr. Payne had allergies, so my mom planted hers on the other side of the house, as a courtesy, I guess. The Paynes were always complaining about something, as I recall. Me, mostly. I bet I broke a window in that house at least twice every baseball season growing up."

"It's a nice little house," she said, taking a few more steps toward the back door, glancing at the considerably bigger house next door. It wouldn't have surprised her to find out that the fence had been erected as a courtesy to the Paynes as well—though why the second gate opened into her yard, she had no idea. Easier baseball retrieval?

"You haven't lived here long. Someone else owned it the last time I was here, for my dad's funeral."

"No. Not long," she said, taking several more steps away.

"You've done a lot of work," he said again, running out of things to say. Pointing here and there, he added, "Painted it. Put the garden in."

She was redecorating the interior too. He'd seen her hauling in buckets of paint and small pieces of furniture. One night, he'd watched her go up and down a ladder a hundred times to paint the ceiling in her dining room, the window of which faced his across the double driveway. But of course, it was still too early in their relationship for him to admit that he'd been spying on her.

"If you ever need any help with anything, I'm usually around."

"Thank you."

He laughed. "I'll bet you're thinking that I should probably work on my own place before I offer to help with yours, huh?"

She had no *nice* comment to make on the subject, he could see. But instead of letting her off easy, he waited for her to say something. Anything.

"That's up to you, Mr. . . . um . . . But it was nice of you to offer."

"Hammond. Scott Hammond. And I meant it. I'd be glad to help out."

"I know," she said, having heard his name a hundred times over the past few weeks, she couldn't believe she'd forgotten it. Though, there didn't seem to be much in her mind at the moment anyway, aside from his smile. "I mean, thank you. It's been nice meeting you, Mr. Ha—"

"Scotty."

Her smile was small as she opened the screen door. She nodded. "Scotty. I'm glad we met."

He wasn't what you'd call a firm believer in love at first sight—lust maybe, not love. But he had a certain instinct about women that rarely disenchanted him. This same intuition was at present on its toes, caroling a Gregorian chant and dancing a jig.

"Are you really?" he asked, unexpectedly. She stared at him, her bright eyes curious and surprised. "Glad we met? Throwing trash in your yard, and sending Bert over to meet you was only a ploy to get your attention. I won't go to all that trouble anymore . . . if there's another way to get you to talk to me."

What a strange man, she thought, and yet rather than run inside and lock the doors, she let the screen door swing closed.

"To get my attention?"

"Sure. It's not like a man moves in next door to a beautiful woman every day. And I couldn't exactly stroll up the walk and knock on your door to deliver one of my usual lines, so I thought I'd do something . . . neighborly. But not like borrow a cup of sugar, because that would make it seem like I'd be pestering you for groceries all the time. And not like bake you a cake, because I'm not very good at that stuff. I'd have shoveled your walk if it were snowing, but it's summer and, well, the trash was handy. In fact, it's been the same cans and wrappers for a week now."

"I see," she said thoughtfully. "And now that you have my attention, is there a point you'd like to make?"

He loved a direct, plain-speaking woman. He really did.

"Yes. I think we should be friends."

"Friends," she repeated.

The way he was looking at her was a lot more than friendly. She didn't know many men, but she knew his type. Big, hunky flirt. High on ego, low on gray matter. Putting aside his dog and his trash and the general state of his house, she'd been willing to give her new neighbor a chance. But now . . . ?

"Definitely friends. Can't have too many friends, right?"

This time the smile reached her eyes . . . and took his breath away. Those first stirrings of desire whipped themselves to a frenzy.

"Actually, Scott, you *can* have too many friends. As a matter of fact, I find myself in that exact predicament at this very moment. You may have to wait until someone I know disowns me or dies."

He smiled back at her undaunted. He also loved a challenge.

"I've waited a whole week just to talk with you. I guess it's a good thing that I'm a patient man."

"Maybe. But I should warn you, most of my friends are young, forgiving, and very healthy."

"I've noticed."

She gave him a sharp look.

"The little kids going in and out," he said quickly. "Your students. When the window's open I can hear them during their violin lessons. You're a very tolerant teacher. Me, I'd be tempted to put a couple of them out of their misery. Friday's two-o'clock lesson is the worst. What a noise."

She didn't mean to, but she chuckled, thinking of poor Levy's little tin ear. "The lessons were his mother's idea. He'd much rather be playing soccer."

"He's probably better at it too."

An awkward moment passed as they realized they were sharing an amusement. He was pleased, she was mildly annoyed.

It wasn't that she didn't like her new neighbor. She found him acceptable, she supposed, having known a few that were worse in New York and Seattle. Likable even, in some vague, loose fashion. But he'd already admitted to having his "usual lines" for meeting women, that the dog and the trash were simply attention-getters. She'd have to be as dumb as a tick on a dead dog not to see his intentions—the smile, the look, the flattery, the manner.

And they might have worked on someone else, she conceded, pegging him literally as a handsome devil.

"I'm sure Levy would appreciate your understanding," she said, opening the screen door again. "However, it isn't yours he needs." She hesitated. "I hope murder isn't your answer for all untalented students."

Ah-ha! So she did know who he was and why he'd

come back to Tylerville. If she was plugged into the local gossip circuit, *that* would explain her extraordinary lack of curiosity. In fact, if she was plugged into the local gossip circuit, she already knew more than he wanted her to.

He turned up the intensity of his smile, the dimples were guaranteed to charm. "No. Actually, I only murder the students who remind me too much of me at their age. Then it's self-preservation."

She nodded, believing him entirely, and tried not to smile as she turned to go inside.

"Hey. Wait a second. What about older friends?" He made an upward hand gesture and looked hopeful. "Taller friends?"

"Sorry. No vacancies," she said, walking inside. She giggled, but didn't realize it.

"Wait. Come back. Your name. What's your name? All your mailbox says is Miller. What's your first name? What should I call you?"

It would have been so simple just to close the door, or to poke her head out and give him her name. But something crazy and impulsive rose up inside her.

She pushed the screen door open, her heart fluttering wildly, and smiled back at his elated expression. "Call me . . ." she said slowly, "Ms. Miller."

The expression on Scotty's face when he turned from the fence would have alarmed a wiser woman. Getting to know *Ms. Miller* had escalated from a clear challenge to a personal quest in a split second. It wouldn't be enough now merely to meet her and see what happened between them. Oh no. Too late for that. He liked her. She was aloof, spunky, quick-witted. It was his new and overpowering belief that in the middle of a heartbeat, he may have fallen hopelessly and totally in love with her.

It was almost like all the poets said it would be—that when you finally fell in love angels would sing and the earth would move. They didn't, of course, but *something* had changed. Something had broken loose, snapped, rotated, altered itself inside him, and he *knew*. He knew she was different, knew she'd make a difference in his life.

He whistled all afternoon, fairly certain that he'd be dancing on the fringes of her mind for the rest of the day—he knew his women. He also suspected she was looking out her windows more often than before and that she was smiling every time she shook her head at his cheeky behavior.

Nope. None of that would have surprised him. However, he'd have been blown clean out of his sneakers to know that he was inadvertently compounding her disapproval and tampering with fate that afternoon when his cleanup crew arrived.

TWO

"Aw! Will you look at that," Gus said to her four walls, appalled, standing well hidden in the shadows of the room. "Flirting with me this morning and now *this* in the afternoon. Not one beautiful woman, but two. Cutoffs and halter tops . . . probably a leg man," she muttered, craning her neck to watch the women climb the steps to the front door, standing bug-eyed and openmouthed when each received a hug and a quick kiss from him—on the mouth. He obviously had a great affection for both women, and it tied her stomach in knots.

"Kinky as a corkscrew." She should have guessed it. Though why he should be any different from the other men she attracted, couldn't be reasoned. Liars, cheaters, playboys every one. Take Nelson Forge, for example. His approach to love and romance was soft music, soft lights, and soft-soaping.

"Well, not this time, Mr. Scott Hammond. *Baby*,"

using Nelson's most sickening endearment. "I've been around this block before," she said, walking head high, spine stiff into the kitchen for a glass of lemonade.

As a rule she limited lessons to two a day, finding more than that to be a strain on her overtrained nerves. But that particular Saturday she had three violin lessons to give, as Molly Bennett had to make up a lesson due to a conflict with a birthday party the day before. Each was a trial to her patience and a test of her dedication. Not because one child was a beginner and the other two hadn't practiced, but because of Scott Hammond.

First, it was irritating that the odd mix of oldies, rap, and contemporary rock music went suddenly silent in the open doors and windows when ten-year-old Andrew Betz arrived for his lesson. Granted, it was considerate, but she would have much preferred that he *not* pay so much attention to the comings and goings at her house.

Later, she had to deal with, "Jeez, Ms. Miller. It sounds like they're having a party next door, doesn't it?"

She refused to turn to the window Andrew was leaning sideways to look through. The female shrieks and laughter coming from the next house were not only highly provocative and indicative of an orgy taking place, they were . . . well, embarrassing. He had no shame. And the women, clearly, had no pride. Such a ruckus.

"Will you two knock it off," she heard Scott

Hammond's distinctively low male voice saying. "If you two think you're getting away from me this quickly, think again. We haven't finished in the bedroom yet."

She cringed, her eyes darting to Andrew to check on his level of awareness as her skin flushed hot and pink with chagrin.

"You know, Andrew," she said, striving to keep her voice calm and detached. "When I played with the Philharmonic in New York there were all sorts of people around me playing lots of different instruments, making lots of different sounds, doing different things. Sometimes it could be very distracting so I had to learn to concentrate. I had to learn to block out other noises and other people and focus on my instrument, the sounds I was making, what I was doing. Let's you and I practice that this afternoon, shall we?"

Then there was Molly Bennett's giggling. . . .

"What's so funny, Molly? Do the vibrations in the strings tickle your fingers? That's common in the beginning, later those vibrations will tell you—"

She stopped when Molly giggled again, this time without playing the violin. She also noticed that Molly was looking over her shoulder, through the window. She turned her head quickly to find Scott Hammond in a window directly across from hers, playing an invisible violin, his movements large and elaborate like a mime in a park. When he finally caught her watching him, he stopped, put a hand in the air as if he were going to swear an oath, and waved

at her with a huge smile, dimples flashing mischie-
vously.

She turned back to Molly.

"You know, Molly, when I played with the Philharmonic in New York there were all sorts of people
around me playing lots of different instruments, making lots of different sounds . . ."

The worst of it came with Mrs. Mutrux, the minister's wife, when she arrived to pick up their son Stephen.

"That's it for today, Stevie," she said, closing his
music books and handing them to him. "Try to remember to keep your head up, use good posture, and
get plenty of extension on your bow. That way the
music will be smooth and not choppy, and each note
will sing out long and pretty for you."

"I think a trumpet would be easier to play than
this old thing," Stevie told her unabashedly.

"Maybe. But every instrument takes practice.
Even the trumpet." She looked at his mother, who
was half in and half out the front door, her attention
directed at the house next door. Naturally, there was
more shrieking and screaming and laughing going on,
but she had long since closed up all her windows, and
it was muffled until now. "Six months was our deal,
remember? If you still don't like the violin by then,
I'll speak with your mother about a trumpet, okay?"

"Okay," he said.

"Stevie's doing very well," she said, getting to her
feet with a sinking feeling that she might have to
apologize for whatever Mrs. Mutrux was watching.

"He needs to set aside a special time each day for practice and work on his form . . . a little . . . and . . ."

Her voice trailed off when she joined the preacher's wife in the doorway and saw what she was seeing—Scott Hammond and the two beautiful women in a water fight on the front lawn.

"Oh dear," she muttered.

"You, too, huh?" Carrie Mutrux asked, glancing at her briefly. "I've known him nearly all my life and he never changes." She smiled wistfully. "I had a crush on him in kindergarten, and as much as I love my husband, I can't really say my feelings for him have changed much since then."

Gus frowned and took a closer look at the minister's wife. A pretty lady with average features, better known for her practical thinking and dedication and hard work toward her husband's church than for her own piety. She looked sensible and sane.

"When he got married and moved away . . ." She shook her head. "I'm so glad he's back," she went on. "It just feels right, you know?"

"Not exactly," she said, taking another look at the melee next door, then pulling back out of sight. She refused to give him any more attention than he deserved—which was none at all.

Mrs. Mutrux smiled at her. "Small towns," she said. "They're chock-full of traditions, and usually for a good reason. When something works, it works. And the Hammonds work here in Tylerville. Always have. Before Mr. Kingsley was principal at the high school,

Joe Hammond was. When he retired . . . well, Mr. Kingsley wasn't Joe Hammond. He wasn't as involved. Didn't have the energy or drive or enthusiasm Joe had, and some of the life went out of it. . . . Not just the high school. The whole community. Tylerville isn't much good for anything but raising families and retiring. Joe had everyone involved in the school system—with the kids, you know? They were number one in his book, and unless Scotty has changed a great deal, he'll make them number one again."

"You think so?"

"Oh, yes. When Scotty agreed to be principal at the high school, you could just," she wiggled head to toe, "*feel* everyone's excitement."

Gus took another quick peek out the door, then looked at the woman as if she'd lost her mind completely.

"*That* Scott Hammond?"

"Yes. Isn't he wonderful? I assume the two of you have met?"

"Oh, yes."

"Stephen, honey? Are you ready?" she asked her son, not taking her gaze off her childhood crush. "Really, Augusta, you won't believe the difference he'll make around here. There's just something about the Hammonds that makes you want to follow their lead. They're all that way. Born leaders. Very civic-minded."

This time, when she passed her skeptical expression beyond the doorway to make sure they were talking about the same person, he was waiting for her.

Hose running in an arch to the ground, he lifted his free hand in the air and started waving.

"Carrie Mutrux, that you?" he shouted, loud enough for the entire neighborhood to hear. "Get yourself over here and let me take a look at you. You sick of being married to that dull old preacher yet?"

"Not yet," she said, heading down the steps with Stevie in tow. "But when I am, you'll be the first to know. You heathen."

She held the screen door open and watched as Scott Hammond and the minister's wife hugged and kissed and hugged again. When they were *finally* finished, he stooped and said something to Stevie, then he and the boy both turned to look at Gus.

"Afternoon, Ms. Miller," he said, smiling that smile. "Hope we weren't making too much noise."

Go to hell sprang to her lips, but there was the minister's wife and child to consider.

"Not at all." She hesitated. "Looks like a fine day for a water fight."

"Care to join us?"

"Not today, thanks. See you next week, Stevie," she said, stepping back inside and closing the door.

"What is the matter with this town? *That* man? Principal of the high school?"

"Gus, you're overreacting," her sister told her over the phone a few minutes later. "Alan says Scotty

Hammond is as good as they come. And I've read his résumé. He's a little overqualified if you ask me, for such a small town."

"Lydia, the man is perverted," she said, flat out. "He's been cavorting with two half-naked women all afternoon."

"Two?" A brief pause. "Well, who could blame them. Isn't he cute?"

"Lydia!" Was she the only person getting a clear image of this terrible picture?

"Well, he is. And if you'd come to dinner with Howard two weeks ago when I begged you to, you could have met him properly. In an official capacity, instead of over the back fence."

"You invited me to have dinner with Howard Munce and the school board, to meet the new high school principal. You made it sound almost as exciting as constipation. Why didn't you tell me he was going to be my next-door neighbor?"

"I didn't know he was planning to be. He was staying with one of his sisters at the time and didn't mention where he planned to live, or I would have told you."

"One of his sisters? How many are there?" She stretched to look out a window, noting a sudden silence in the neighborhood. Nothing.

"Um," her sister hummed distractedly, always busy doing two things at once, even on the telephone. "He has seven or eight of them here in town. All with different last names because they're all married, but I understand the family was quite large and very close.

The father was the high school principal years ago, even before Alan and I moved here."

"You know," Gus said thoughtfully. "Of the two of us, you're definitely the more talkative. In fact, I don't know anyone who talks *more* than you, except Mother. And yet, you've been remarkably secretive about this man."

Lydia giggled. "Have I? Maybe that's because I was thinking that if things didn't work out between you and Howard, I might hook you up with Scotty Hammond."

She groaned. "Oh, God." Now she was getting a headache. "Lydia, if you don't stop trying to attach me to every unattached man in this town, I'm going back to New York. I'll get a counter job at Macy's and play backup in the first coffeehouse that'll take me. *And* I'll tell Mother it was your idea."

"That's rich. She still thinks your move to Tylerville was my fault."

"You're the one with the husband on the school board, and you're the one who recommended me for the job of music director at the elementary school, and you're the one who said you'd smooth things over with her if I came."

"And wasn't I right? Tell me you didn't have fun last year, teaching all those little kids to sing and play recorders and shake tambourines."

"All right. I did. It was fun."

Truth to tell, the best thing to date about coming to Tylerville was the discovery of children. She'd had little to no exposure to them before that time. Now she couldn't seem to get enough of them. She found them open, creative, contagiously happy, and, in general, extremely easy to please.

"And hasn't Mother come around?"

"She's accepted the fact that I'm not good enough to play professionally anymore, yes. But I think she wants me to teach at Yale or Juilliard . . . or even MacPhail. Elementary school chorus and private violin lessons aren't really what she'd define as preserving the arts."

"Of course it is. Who better to preserve it in than children? And how better to serve the community than by instilling an appreciation for music in its young? Answer me that? Your problem—and Mother's problem—is that you take things too literally. You think too big. Little towns, little people, little things are just as important as big towns, big people, and big things. Maybe more."

"And your problem," Gus said, after a few seconds of silent agreement and self-affirmation, "is the same as it's always been. You're too down-to-earth, and you're too often right."

"That's two problems."

"You see, you're right again."

If you pinned her to the mat, Gus would eventually admit that she viewed her attendance at church services more as a tolerable social obligation than anything involving her religious attitudes.

Fact of the matter was she enjoyed being . . .

well, recognized was probably the proper word for it. It was a throwback to her days of being first violinist with the New York Philharmonic and soloist with the Chambers, a rather well-known and elite group of musicians who hired out for private gatherings and exhibitions.

Granted, she was now *Ms. Miller* to the loud church whispers of children, and Augusta to the smiles and friendly greetings of their parents, who knew her as nothing more than a music teacher. But she could remember a time when people she considered to be colleagues and friends couldn't bring themselves to look her in the eye, much less offer her a cheery good-morning.

When she first arrived in Tylerville, she'd sat with Lydia and Alan and their three children as a family in church. It wasn't long after that that Lydia had invited Howard Munce to a family picnic to meet her unmarried sister, or long after *that* that he started feeling obliged to take up the empty space in the pew beside her.

She hadn't lied to Scott Hammond when she'd told him she had an overabundance of friends. There was Howard, of course, a balding forty-something pharmacist who sat on the school board with her brother-in-law and had a tendency to monologue on the pros and cons of allergy therapy versus the frequent use of modern antihistamines, or some equally enthralling controversy. And there was Bill Wexell, the third-grade teacher who lived with his mother and enjoyed the fact that Tylerville was actually a state-designated bird sanctuary. And Louis Green, manager of the local Safeway, who frequently boasted of having the *greenest* produce in town.

All fine men. All eager to please her. All as boring as watching grass grow.

And so it was that she'd taken to eating her lunches in the music room at school and avoiding the third-grade classroom whenever possible, grocery shopping at the A & P, and coming in late to church on Sundays to take the last available seat among strangers—or the second to last available seat as it happened that particular Sunday. The *very* last space was taken by Scott Hammond, who wedged himself in beside her seconds before the service began.

"This couldn't have worked out better," he said, breathless and grinning. Her insides were flipping and spinning. His Sunday best was more than enough to send her pulse racing—but under it was the bare wet chest from the day before, a thin and incredibly sexy line of dark hair straight down the middle of it, disappearing into the waistband of his pants. . . . "I'm usually too lazy to get all dressed up for church, but I saw you out the window, looking as pretty as spring's first rose, and thought I'd give it a try. What do you think?" he asked, since he already had her ogle-eyed attention. "Is this tie okay? All my others are still packed in boxes."

She was speechless. After the day he'd had, he was worried about his tie? And why wasn't she breathing?

She was saved making a comment, one way or the

other, when the congregation stood to sing the first hymn.

"Oops. No more hymnals. I guess we'll have to share," he said, his dark eyes and naughty dimples twinkling happily. "You don't mind, do you?"

She lowered her eyes away, afraid the whole world could see just how much she did mind, and shifted her hands and the open book to the space between them—which he immediately narrowed by turning toward her and leaning close to see the music.

He sang loud in a near perfect tenor voice, pronouncing the words clearly, modeling a devout believer—except when she happened to glance up during the second chorus and he winked at her. If a woman had curves, he had all the angles.

They sat down and there was hardly enough room for his broad shoulders despite the fact that she was all but sitting in the lap of the woman next to her.

"There appears to be more room in the pew behind us," she whispered to him after a quick look over her shoulder.

"Appearances can be deceiving."

"I think you'd be more comfortable back there."

"I'm comfortable here," he said. He wiggled his shoulders closer to hers and smiled when she pushed back. "I like the way your hair smells, by the way." He leaned over a tiny bit, inhaled deeply through his nose, then hummed out a little sigh. "Like a starry summer night."

No one but her could have heard it; still, she went hot all over and focused her eyes on the front of the church. Her pulse was pounding and she was too aware of his upper arm against hers, the scent of his aftershave, his neatly trimmed fingernails and long strong-looking fingers. And the heat. She decided there and then that it should be against the law to hold church services in August without air-conditioning. Truly, it was criminal.

She jumped a foot when he reached over and covered her hand with his—to silence the agitated opening and closing of her hymnal that was distracting the people around them. After a little squeeze he removed his hand, leaving hers scorched and throbbing.

"Nervous?" he muttered under his breath. As a bee in a bottle, if he was any judge.

She cleared her throat softly and ignored him.

"I don't bite."

Ha! She bet he did. Nibbled, most likely. On tender places like necks . . . and maybe breasts . . . and the inside of a woman's thigh . . . and . . . Humph! She wiggled and sat up a little taller. Those two women yesterday would know if he bit or not. Frankly, she didn't care.

Heavens, it was hot.

Suddenly, they were singing again and whole chunks of the service were missing from her mind. She felt so distracted. He had his arm resting along the back of the pew behind her and was breathing down her neck as he sang.

"Move your arm," she said with tight lips. He wrapped it about her shoulders. "*Remove* your arm."

He let it fall to the back of the pew again and continued singing. "People are looking at us."

"I know," he said, close to her ear, his warm breath tickling her cheek. "They're all thinking we're a cute couple."

"Well, we're not," she said, turning her head to glare at him, finding herself nose to nose.

"Not yet," he said, his brown eyes soft, entrancing as a half-remembered tune, his lips a breath away, tempting her.

She would have continued to sing the rest of the song, but she was just too flustered . . . no, too mad. She would have slapped him and stalked out of the church, but she was worried that making a scene would make things worse. She would have put her elbow through his ribs, but she was sure it would make him happy.

She couldn't honestly compliment Reverend Mutrux on his sermon that day. She found it incredibly long and tedious—and she couldn't remember a single word of it. However, that didn't mean she'd fallen asleep. She sang the final hymn with great verve, actually, anticipating the quick escape she had planned.

Having spotted Dorothy Weise, Tylerville's local Avon-Amway-Tupperware representative, across the aisle and two pews back it was a simple matter of timing her exit.

"I want to apologize for yesterday," he said while the last organ note still vibrated off the church walls, afraid she'd get away from him again before they could really talk. "I do know better than to distract children from their lessons. I'm sorry."

"You should be." She was busy putting away the hymnal and gathering up her purse, and didn't look at him—but she did appreciate his remorse. Perhaps his visit to church wasn't a total loss. He did look very fine in his Sunday best. Scrubbed up nicely. Crisp. Clean. Sexy as hell.

"I am," he said, bending low to see her face. "I was wondering . . . I didn't hear you playing last night . . . I . . . please don't be so angry with me that you stop playing your violin," he said in a rush. "I don't know how we got off to a wrong start here, but I'm sure I've done something to offend you. If it's the garbage thing?"

Long personal discussions took a great deal of the casual out of the phrase "casual acquaintance." What she did and how she felt were personal.

"Mr. Ham—Scott," she broke in.

"My close friends call me Scotty."

"Please. I'd like to leave."

"Sure," he said, backing out of the pew but blocking her exit. "I just wanted to apologize and to let you know I really like listening to you play. I mean, I'm sorry if I'm eavesdropping or . . . well, I'm not spying on you, really, it's just that the windows are open and . . . I never knew a violin could sound like that."

"I'm glad it doesn't irritate you. And believe me, I've overcome greater obstacles than you to play my violin. Excuse me, please?"

"I noticed you walked here. Would you like a lift home? I happen to be going that way."

"No. But thanks," she said, nudging him aside before her best chance got away. "Mrs. Weise. How are you?"

Scotty knew Dorothy Weise and automatically panicked, his fight-or-flight instincts acute, until he noticed the glimmer in Gus's eyes.

"Low blow," he muttered under his breath as the woman approached them. A giggle bubbled in her throat.

"Augusta, dear, you look lovely this morning. And all you ever order is the twenty-four ounce Aroma Therapy Bubble Bath. It's obviously working. Looking very refreshed and relaxed this morning."

"Thank you," she said, and without hesitating she added, "Have you met Mr. Hammond? He's recently moved back into his family home, which has stood empty for so long now that, well, you know how dirty things can get when they're neglected. I was going to . . ."

"Oh, my gracious, yes," Dorothy said, feeling the baton in her hand and running with it. "I've known Scotty since he was no bigger than the little end of nothing. You sweet boy, how are you? I heard you were coming back to town." She took hold of his forearm and Gus's heart smiled. He wouldn't be getting away any time soon. "And taking up your daddy's old job no less. I can't tell you how happy I was to hear it."

"Thank you, Mrs.—"

"And that old house of yours. Lord A'mighty. What a terror it must be for you. I can't even imagine the ground-in dust and dirt. This is the worst season of the year for mold and mildew and . . ."

Gus began taking small steps backward, out of the conversation and out of the church. She couldn't stop the chuckle. He deserved this, he really did, she decided, shrugging innocently when he issued her an I'll-get-you-for-this look.

Unconsciously, she fisted the fingers of her left hand and twisted her wrist in a small circle. Round and round—then back in the opposite direction. Actually, she was doing him a favor, she thought, appeasing what little guilt she felt for being so unkind to him. Someday he'd thank her for her disinterest. He would. She wasn't a quick roll in the hay sort of woman, and anything more . . . well, even if he were looking for more, he wouldn't find it in her.

Disappointing people was what she was good at. It wasn't a motivating force in her life, certainly, but when you've disappointed enough people—despite all your best efforts to do exactly the opposite—you eventually begin to recognize the pattern of your existence. Disappointment was Augusta's pattern. So far, she'd been a massive disillusionment to everyone she'd ever cared about, including herself.

Except for Lydia, of course.

She watched her sister—over Howard's right shoulder—later that afternoon. With baby Todd on her hip, she flipped hamburgers on the grill and warned her two older children to beware of the flowers as they kicked a soccer ball around the yard. She was, without a doubt, the most stubborn, blindly devoted, and tolerant sister ever born, Gus surmised.

Or else she was just plain stupid.

She managed never to disappoint *any*one. Not her husband. Not her children. Not her sister. Not her teachers. Not her friends. Not her . . .

". . . and then Scotty Hammond joined the team and—"

"What?" Gus asked, falling from her reverie so unexpectedly she felt dizzy. Yes. Yes, they were still in her tidy little backyard. It was her turn to hostess the Sunday barbecue. "Who did you say?"

"Scott Hammond," Howard said. "Lydia was saying he moved back into his parents' house, next door to you." He motioned toward the big house with his head.

"He did. Yes. But I thought we were talking about asthma."

Lydia and Alan laughed. "Forgive her, Howard. The mind of a true artist is never really where it's supposed to be," her sister said, shaking her head. "It's just sort of around, in the vicinity, dropping in now and again to catch up on the conversation. Pay attention, Gus."

Howard chuckled good-naturedly. Alan left to get drinks for the children.

"We were talking about asthma, Augusta," Howard said, carefully pronouncing all three syllables of her name. "Larry Masterson had terrible asthma growing up, but he was a terrific basketball player, except that he tired quickly. He was a couple years older than Scotty, but when he—Scotty—finally made the team, the two of them played off each other like pros. Scotty did all the rebounding and running around and Larry sank every ball he got his hands on. They went to the state championship games two years in a row."

"This is the mayor Larry Masterson?" Gus questioned. She'd never seen the man, but had heard a great deal about him from Alan and Lydia.

"The very same. He and Scotty were like brothers growing up. Rumor has it, it was Larry who got Scotty to come back and take over at the high school."

"You're a big Hammond fan, too, I take it."

Why someone didn't simply canonize the man, she didn't know.

He took a plate with a hamburger on it from Lydia, who was giving her sister the eye to behave herself, as she seated the children around the small backyard picnic table. Alan was backing his way out the door with their drinks.

"Everything the man touches turns to gold," Howard said in his very serious way. "It's hard not to like him."

Not for her.

"Lydia tells me there are several sisters and they all still live here in town."

"Yes, yes, they do."

"Well, how many are there exactly? Lydia says there are six or seven of them."

"No no. There were a bunch of them all right, but only five sisters, with Scotty born smack in the middle of them. Big, busy family, volunteering for this, running that, seems like they're everywhere. I'm a year or two older than Donna, so I didn't know them well. It's hard to keep track of them all."

In an eerie, unexpected moment the wind stopped rustling the leaves in the trees and the insects ceased buzzing and no one spoke as a clear, steady whistling drifted over the fence and filled the air around them like a . . . a rain cloud, was her first thought, her heart leaping into her throat then hitting hard somewhere near her feet.

The others didn't appear to be particularly put out by this untimely development. Eyes and heads turned to the fence as the snappy, happy tune drew closer. She could tell they were expecting Scott Hammond's face to appear over the five-foot fence at any moment—but was she the only one holding her breath? And just exactly how uncool would it be to shoo *him* away with a broom?

The whistling stopped abruptly, and the anticipation mounted rapidly. They waited. No sound. No Scotty. Their gazes drifted back to the table, to one another, then back to the fence.

Alan, normally a great brother-in-law and the manager of the local fan factory that was one of the major veins of Tylerville's economic structure, was, unfortunately, a get-it-done sort of fellow.

"Scotty Hammond?" he bellowed. "That you over there?"

"Why, yes, it is," he replied, a little too casually to Gus's thinking. "Who's asking?" he said moments before his face rose, dimpled and curious, over the fence. "Well, look at this," he said—and she was sure he had been for some time. "Howard. Alan. Lydia. Hi, kids," he said, waving to the children. "Ms. Miller. I thought I smelled barbecue out here."

"Have you eaten yet?" Lydia, the dumbest sister in the world, asked. "Come join us. There's plenty."

He made a feeble attempt to appear humble before he said, "I don't want to intrude. This looks like a family dinner."

"Don't be silly," Lydia said. "We'd love to have you. Wouldn't we, Gus?"

It took her so long to answer that everyone was watching when she finally nodded and muttered, "I guess."

"In that case, I'd love to," he said, beaming. "I'll put Bert in the house."

"Oh, bring him along," Lydia said, pretending not to notice the look her sister was sending her. "We love dogs."

"Well, great. Come on, Bert. You mind your manners now."

"Lydia," she growled without moving her lips.

"Well, the poor man lives alone. He needs to eat," she whispered back. In self-defense she slid closer to Jake, her middle child, in case Gus planned to throw something at her.

"He has a thousand sisters to eat with," she groused.

"Don't you like him?" Howard asked. He shot a quizzing glance to Alan—as if there was something clearly wrong with her if she didn't like Scott Hammond. "I've never met anyone who didn't like him."

"I hardly know the man," she said. "Which makes inviting him to Sunday dinner a little awkward."

Howard smiled at that. "Oh. Is that all? Well, he'll fix that soon enough. I never met anyone who didn't like him. Everything the man touches turns to gold. It's hard not to like him."

Great. Howard was repeating himself and the space between her eyes was filling with a pressure that promised to be a full-blown headache before dessert. The evening was taking on the dimensions of a wide-awake nightmare.

THREE

"This is really nice of you to invite me over," Scotty was saying as he flipped the latch on the garden gate—which was something else that annoyed her. There was no way to lock him out from her side of the fence. "I've been working all day and I'm starving. The smell of barbecue in the air has been driving me and Bert crazy for the past hour. I was just now going after fast food, but this is much better," he said, walking across her neatly trimmed grass, Bert lumbering behind. "Nothing beats home cooking. Right, Howard?"

"That's for sure. Not when you're single," he agreed, smiling brightly at him. "I look forward to Sunday all week long."

Scott turned his whole face into a frown and tried to look confused.

"Just Sunday? Aren't you and Ms. Miller . . . ? Oh. You're not one of those weekend-only cooks, are you, Ms. Miller? My mom used to tell my sisters that there was no shorter way to a man's heart than through his stomach."

The rain cloud burst and silence fell like water in a monsoon as eyes turned to her, waiting for her comment to his remark—which wasn't about cooking at all, but her relationship with Howard.

"Well," she said, clearing her throat. "I'm sure your mother was correct. I understand you have several married sisters here in town, and I'm sure they're all excellent cooks. In fact, I bet you could—"

"That's right, I do," he said, cutting her off with a huge smile. "All but Donna, that is. Well, she's a great cook and she's married, she just doesn't live here in Tylerville anymore."

"How fascinating."

"How is Donna?" Howard asked, looking too eager to know.

"Just great. Saw her and her brood of kids a couple weeks ago. She's just great. Sure do miss having her around though."

"Me too," Howard said, so wistfully that when he realized what he'd said, he blushed, and for the first time in perhaps . . . ever, he had everyone's full attention. "I mean . . . well, she was younger than I was, but I had this . . . well, a little crush on her in high school." He laughed self-consciously, shook his head, and took a bite of his hamburger.

Scotty chuckled sympathetically. "You're in good company, Howard. The streets of this town are littered with hearts my sisters have broken. Pains me to see it. And I never could understand it."

Howard shook his head and held up his hand, chewing and swallowing quickly. "You're their brother," he said, stating the obvious with some authority. "Brothers never understand the attraction other men have toward their sisters."

"Well, I understand it now, of course, but back then . . ." he said, his voice softening a bit with affection. He came to stand beside Gus at the end of the table, reaching over her to take the paper plate and juicy hamburger Lydia was handing to him. "It was tough being the only boy. Thanks. Looks great. It was just me and my dad and that house full of women."

"How's it going over there," Alan asked, passing the potato salad. "I smelled paint all the way out in the driveway when we got here. Need any help?"

Paint? She hadn't smelled any paint—other than that of her own redecorating. But since he was still standing beside her and his hands were in her line of vision, she could see that there were little specks and smudges of paint on his hands that hadn't come off when he'd washed.

She glanced up and he looked down at her expectantly. Clearly, he had every intention of sitting next to her and wouldn't move until she slid over, closer to Howard. With Lydia, Alan, and two of the children on the other side of the table, and one child and Howard and her on the other, she was forced to make room for him.

"You know," he said cheerfully, sitting down beside her and taking up an incredible amount of room, "I'd forgotten how big that house really is." He chuckled and reached for the ketchup, his arm brushing hers and coming back to rest against her ribs. She squirmed closer to Howard, whose body didn't seem to generate quite so much electrical energy. "I could paint and paper in that place from now till doomsday and never be finished. I don't know how my dad did it all those years. A couple of my sisters came over yesterday to help out."

"Those were your sisters?" she asked, embarrassing herself. "I mean, so those were your sisters. I . . . I'd been wondering if I knew any of them. I guess . . . I don't."

If she were queen for a day, she would have had the grin he gave her slapped clean off his face, the knowing look in his eyes put out with hot pokers. As it was, she turned her attention to her food and cursed the heat in her cheeks—not that she could possibly eat anything with her heart beating so fast. Was he brushing his thigh against hers on purpose?

"You will," he said, deciding then and there that she was the cutest thing ever when she was flustered. Addressing the others he said, "They're pretty good help when you can get them to work. But all they wanted to do yesterday was play and giggle and talk about when we were kids." He took a big bite out of his burger and hummed his pleasure.

"It must be nice, coming from a big family like that," Lydia said, looking at her own children as they ate their food and threw potato chips at each other, then to Gus. "There was only the two of us and . . . well, I was raised different from Augusta." She smiled sympathetically. "She was gifted, so instead of a childhood, she got trained."

Once again, the spotlight had swung around the table to focus on Gus. She sighed loudly and laid her fork down with a resigned shrug of her shoulders. She could tell they were going to discuss her private, personal life come hell, high water, flood, avalanche, hurricane. . . .

It was one of those afternoons.

"It wasn't any easier on you, being raised the way we were," she said, feeling Scott Hammond's attention span increasing tenfold. Under the table she fisted the fingers of her left hand and twisted her wrist around in a small circle. Around and around—then back in the opposite direction. "Our mother believes that it is every individual's duty and privilege to be of some sort of service to the community they live in." She glanced at Howard, who was just as attentive but much less threatening somehow. "According to her everyone has a talent or a gift for something and it should be developed extensively and given back to the world if possible. Failing that, to your race or society or your state or city." She laughed softly. "Your ability to contribute gets progressively smaller with your failures, believe me." She smiled at Lydia and chuckled in spite of the heaviness in her chest. "She'll appoint herself cruise director when we finally commit her to a retirement home, you know."

Lydia laughed. "All those poor old people, licking

envelopes and picketing cosmetic companies in their walkers and wheelchairs, taking buses out into the country to pick up trash along the highway. Finish eating, Eric," she said to the child across from her. "Remember when everyone dropped out of Mother's troop of Girl Scouts and joined up with Mrs. Macaby's group because she insisted they all ban Christmas trees and ask their parents to buy living trees they could plant in their yards after the holidays?"

Gus laughed too. "What about the time she showed up at your school with all those dogs she was trying to save from the pharmaceutical labs?"

"That wasn't funny," Lydia said, chuckling anyway. "Mother can be very intimidating sometimes. Well, always really," she said, trying to explain to Howard and Scotty. "Those kids didn't stand a chance of telling her their own parents would kill them for bringing home some stray dog from the pound. They *had* to take them home or suffer my mother's eternal displeasure. Which no one in their right mind would ever elect to do."

"Nanny isn't coming to visit, is she?" asked Eric, Lydia's oldest and most sober son. Gus recognized the concerned frown on his face as something she felt every time the phone rang.

"No, sweetie. She was just here a few weeks ago. Remember?"

"Yeah," he said, slipping away from the table. "I just thought she was coming again."

Jake followed Eric over to hang on and pester the

woebegone looking Bert, who thought of children as huge fleas, one of the many indignities a dog suffered in his life.

Lydia watched them, then shook her head and stood to clear their places.

"She stood outside the front door and put a leash in every hand she could grab hold of and all the dogs were gone by the time the principal got there to stop her," she said, finishing the story as if she were simply remembering aloud, her voice impassive.

Without exchanging a word or a glance the sisters recalled a multitude of crimes committed against them as children. Moments of deep embarrassment, feeling weak and defenseless against their mother's stronger will. The frustration of being without control of their own destinies, of bending constantly to the whims and attitudes of a woman with fierce opinions and ambitions.

"I remember that was the first time I actually felt lucky to be away at school," Gus said absently.

"What happened to all the dogs?" Howard asked, finished with his meal. "Did the parents let the kids keep them?"

Lydia shrugged. "Either that or they sent them back to the pound, I guess. I was pretty young and didn't hear much more about it—except for the way the other kids would look at me after that, and how they walked way out of Mother's reach whenever she was around."

She offered Scott a third hamburger, which he refused with a smile while he reached for more potato salad. He met Gus's eyes with his, silently searching and questioning as he leaned in front of her.

"She sounds like quite a character," Howard said, much to Gus's relief.

It was much easier to answer his casual questions than avoid Scott's probing glances, or to be left with a moment of silence in which to ponder the warmth of his body against hers, or to enjoy the smell of his aftershave or to admire the strength and grace of his hand movements.

"Yes," she said, standing rather suddenly, deliberately insinuating a note of humor in her voice. "I'd say character describes her well enough, wouldn't you, Liddy?"

"Oh yeah. For lack of a kinder expression," she said, smiling at her sister as she set her plate atop Alan's before taking them both away. "She was hard to live with, whether you were there or not," she added.

Gus took Howard's plate in a similar manner and started toward the trash cans beside the small garage.

"So, the two of you didn't really grow up together," Howard said. "I remember Augusta saying once that she loved *remeeting* you."

"Did she?" Lydia looked pleased. "It's been like that, hasn't it, Gus?"

She nodded, turning back to the party. "While Liddy was being indoctrinated into civil service, I got lucky with a knack for music."

"A knack?" her sister asked, clearing away condiments. "You picked up Daddy's violin when you were four, and there wasn't anyone left in Seattle who could teach you anything by the time you were ten. Eight, really, because that last teacher came all the way up from San Francisco to work with you."

"You know," she said, feeling profoundly uncomfortable as her wrist throbbed and her full stomach twisted itself into nervous knots, "I'll bet Mr. . . . ah, Scott's plans for the new school year are a lot more interesting than our ancient history. There was a regular buzz about it after church this morning."

"Was there?" he said, surprised. Half a glance told her that he knew she was uneasy. It was nice of him to take the heat off her for a while. "I'm sorry I missed it. An opportunity to be the center of attention isn't something I'd generally miss out on. Which reminds me," he said, with a direct look at Gus. "If any of you need any cleaning products, I have a small truckload arriving sometime next week."

He listened to the swift vibrant movement of Vivaldi's The Four Seasons with his eyes closed, totally unaware of its title but deeply moved by the passion with which it was being played. Soft as falling snow. Hot and intense as the summer sun. Whimsical as leaves in the winds of autumn.

A knack for music.

He sent the porch swing rocking with a one-legged shove and rested a hand over the tight spot in his chest.

Ms. Augusta Miller had a knack for music, he

thought. Her face in a dozen different expressions flashed through his mind. Laughing. Thoughtful. Teasing. Sad. There was more to her music than a simple knack, and more to her than her music.

Finagling an invitation to dinner had been child's play, a means of being near her and annoying her at once. He hadn't known it would change the feeling in his chest from a flutter to an ache. Hadn't known that tiny morsels of information about her would leave him ravenous for more. Never guessed that sitting beside her would make everything smell like a field of wildflowers for hours afterward.

He'd arrived home after church itching inside his skin with a need to see her again. He'd tried to paint the hall walls for a while and let the paint dry on his brush watching her and her guests from the upstairs window—hating harmless old Howard, despite her obvious lack of interest in him.

And that was something else. . . . Though he could tell she wasn't as immune to him as she was to Howard, she made it too clear she wasn't interested in developing *their* relationship beyond a "Howdy, neighbor" stage.

"I don't suppose I could interest you in giving me some gardening advice?" he'd asked when they found themselves alone at the picnic table picking at the leftover watermelon. Lydia and the baby were trying to snooze in a shaded lawn chair several feet away; Alan and Howard were strolling the tree-lined sidewalk in front of the house with the other two boys.

"No, I don't suppose you could," she said, her voice bland and disinterested.

"I'd do all the work. I'm just not sure which plants to plant where. You know, full shade, bright light. That sort of thing."

"Borrow a book from the library."

He glanced quickly at Lydia and found he didn't care if she heard what he was about to say or not.

"You're not going to make this easy for me, are you?"

She looked up from the melon rind she was slowly forking with bored rhythmic motions. "What? Your gardening?" She set the fork down. "Why should I?"

He shook his head. "Getting to know you. You aren't going to make it easy."

She lowered her eyes from his and sighed, placing her hands under the table. "There's not much to know, Mr. . . . ah, Scott."

"Why do you find it so hard to call me Scotty?"

Now she glanced at her sister and apparently came to the same decision he had. "Calling you Scotty would make you seem like a friend. I don't want or need any more friends. I told you that."

"Okay. Then would you say you're more interested in Howard's friendship than you are in mine?"

She frowned. "No. Not really. He's more a friend of Alan's and Lydia's."

"But you call him Howard. Why can't you call me Scotty?"

She looked as if she wanted to argue with him, but then she chuckled and shook her head. "All right," she said, reaching for the plate of seeds and juice in front of him. "I give up. Scotty it is."

Feeling ridiculously victorious, he reached out for her arm and was about to detain her long enough to get her to smile at him when the tips of his fingers felt the soft ridge of skin on the inside of her wrist.

Without thinking, with no thought at all, he turned her hand palm up. Pink and shiny, the scar across her wrist stood out against her pale skin as a sign of despair and abdication. His shock must have registered in his face when he looked at her, because she snatched her hand away from him, hid it under the table, and glared at him as if he'd violated her.

"I'm sorry," he said, quickly and softly, not knowing what else to say. "I . . ."

"Don't jump to conclusions," she said, reaching for his plate a second time with her right hand. "You still don't know anything about me."

But he wanted to, and he would have told her so if she hadn't hurried away with the plates and then managed to avoid him for the rest of the time he'd stayed—playing with the kids, talking to Alan and Howard for a while, and then to Lydia about the upcoming school year.

He rubbed the tightness in his chest as he sat in his porch swing and opened his eyes. The overwhelming urge to go to her had him sitting up, leaning forward to brace his arms on his knees, then lacing his fingers together in frustration.

If he were King of the World he'd first tear down the fence in the backyard and then her front door, so there would be no physical barriers between them. He'd walk straight into her house and into her soul. He'd take her in his arms and hold her. Tight. Kiss her until she was too weak to resist him any longer and then he'd go right on kissing her until she felt no more pain, no more regrets, no more of whatever she'd been feeling when she slit her own wrist. If he were King of the World.

He sighed heavily and sagged back in the swing, combing the fingers of both hands through his hair. This was a hell of a time for him to be falling in love with a needy woman.

A needy woman? She was as ornery and stubborn as a mule.

She was a Chinese puzzle with no beginning or end, no rhyme or reason. Nothing about her made sense in his head . . . and yet everything about her spoke to his heart.

A new school year would be starting in less than three weeks. He had a new job to prepare for, a house to get in order, a life for himself and his daughter to arrange. Now was not the time to be falling in love.

But he was. And he knew it.

He glanced over at the house next door when the music slowly faded to an end. The last note floated in the air to be picked up and used as a first note by the crickets and night bugs, as they began their own nightly recital. He felt a strange sort of relief, as if his mind was suddenly his own again.

He made a concerted effort to make a mental list of to-dos, frowned over the decision to paint Chloe's room pink and surprise her or to let her pick out her own paint. He nearly broke a sweat steering his thoughts away from the woman next door and toward anything pertinent to his own life.

Restless and scattered, he finally stood to go inside—maybe paint a couple more walls before he went off to toss and turn in bed, to dream of touching her, to ponder on the taste of her, to imagine her whispers in the dark. . . .

"Damn," he muttered, opening the screen door and hearing another slam closed nearby.

Vivaldi's Four Seasons always made her melancholy, even though it was a favorite she loved playing. Maybe it had something to do with time passing and life changing, she ruminated as she slipped out the kitchen door to restore her little garden to its well-ordered, pre–nephews-and-neighbor's-dog state of tidiness.

She smiled a little, thinking of the boys and that huge beast, so mild-tempered and tolerant. And to think he'd frightened her, she chuckled softly, folding lawn chairs and stacking them neatly inside the garage door.

The back porch light glinted off a soda can. Picking it up, she was tempted to toss it over the fence to . . . well, just to do it. To get back at Scott Hammond for making her feel this way. Restless and unfocused. She put the can in a garbage bag with a stray napkin and tied a knot in the top of it.

Scott Hammond. Scotty. His name flirted with her mind as boldly and consistently as he teased her. . . .

"Do you like children," he'd asked her, straight out and direct, breathless from playing human tackle dummy with the boys. She'd just received a sloppy wet kiss for tying Jake's shoe and the question had caught her off guard.

"Of course," she said. "Sure. Most. Depends on the kid, I guess."

"I have a daughter. She's five."

"Eric's almost six," she said, describing the extent of her intimate experience with five-year-olds. "I like kindergarten kids, and first-graders. They're very eager to please."

He nodded, watching her. Something he'd been doing all afternoon. Something that was really getting on her nerves. Was he memorizing her gestures and expressions? Studying her as if she were a research project? Why couldn't he look at her when she wasn't looking back? The way she watched him? He had wonderfully broad shoulders and the nicest backside she'd seen in years, with long, well-shaped legs and . . . Damned if she was going to stare though.

"She stays with me every other weekend," he said.

"That must be hard," she said, thinking of her own childhood without an active father. He'd given up his battle with her mother when she was seven and avoided all three of them whenever possible.

"It is," he said, glancing at the back door as Howard came out of the house and started toward them again. "I hate it. I miss not having her around all the time. The worst part of it is, I think she's handling the separation better than I am."

Now she did stare a little. He was speaking so candidly, looked so vulnerable. It was information she could use against him, hurt him with if she wanted to—but he was trusting her not to.

"I believe women handle divorce better than men do," Howard said, sitting down beside Gus to join the conversation. "I mean, in the overall scheme of things. It's painful for everyone, but it's been my observation that women tend to bounce back faster."

Scotty shook his head. It was his experience that no one handled a divorce very well. "I meant Chloe. She doesn't seem to mind the weekends, it's just the way things are for her. I'm the one who knows things should be different. Wants them to be different. I resent the time I can't be with her."

"But that was another reason why you came back here, wasn't it? To be closer to her?" Howard said, then, as if speaking for the entire town, he added, "We wondered what you'd do, when we heard Janis had moved back to Springfield."

He shrugged, and for an instant she thought she saw shame in his eyes, shame and something else . . . extreme discomfort. Though he was the one who had brought the subject up, perhaps he hadn't meant to discuss it with Howard. He said, "There wasn't anything I could do."

"How will you handle it now?" Howard asked, then chuckled. "When you've been single as long as I have, you come to know all the ins and outs of a divorce and visitation rights. I'm an authority on it, and I've never even been married." He laughed.

Scotty gave him a small smile and seemed reluctant to answer. "Janis and I will meet in the middle, an hour drive for each of us, on Friday nights and Sunday afternoons."

"Your little girl doesn't have allergies, does she?" Gus asked, having a sudden brainstorm, not knowing why she felt so sorry for him, only that she did and wanted to help him, to protect him from any further prying.

"No," he said, looking confused.

"Oh now, you shouldn't sound so sure when you say that, Scotty," Howard warned him, picking up on one of his favorite subjects. "Children can develop allergies overnight. To drugs. To food. They build up an intolerance over a period of time and—zap—it's trips to the allergist twice a month. Or in milder cases many pediatricians recommend treating the symptoms with over-the-counter drugs. . . ."

Several more minutes went by before Scotty's eyes slowly trailed back to her face, the twinkle in them the only outward sign of his knowledge and gratitude of the good deed she'd done. She smiled at him briefly, then lowered her gaze away when she realized they were once again connecting, on a nonverbal level.

Connecting with someone like Scotty Hammond would be a big mistake, she knew. Having had some time to think about it, about his attitudes toward fathering and his sisters and the town of Tylerville, maybe there was more to him than a great smile and a cocky attitude. What a shame. It was so much easier to think of him as a lazy, insincere cad than a responsible man with feelings and principles and ideals.

The picnic table was heavy, and she had to move one end at a time, sort of walk it back to its place beside the garage.

"Wait a second." She heard his voice and jumped a little. "I'll help you."

Why she was surprised to hear his voice and the latch lifting on the gate she didn't know. So many times that evening, in the quiet of her little house, she'd heard his laughter, his voice commenting on a sister or describing his daughter or enthusiastically explaining his plans for the upcoming school year. Several times she'd turned around to see if he was standing behind her. This time he was.

He took several jogging steps across her yard and took up the opposite end of the picnic table. They swung it into place together.

"Thanks," she said, smiling and looking away as he grinned at her, self-satisfied. He was so tickled to have achieved the center of her consideration again, to know he was paramount in her mind for the moment, and to see she wasn't oblivious to him.

Oblivious, indeed. Her pulse was racing and her mouth had gone dry. She might have met a stranger in a dark alley with less anxiety.

"My pleasure. My house may need paint, and my dog and I invite ourselves to dinner, but we can also be very handy to have around."

"So I see," she said, trying to smile again, her face feeling stiff. "Is it also true that you can leap tall buildings in a single bound and that everything you touch turns to gold?"

"Yes," he said, and he didn't hesitate to add, "I also hang the moon and the stars . . . at least that's what I tell Chloe."

She gave an amused but nervous laugh. Howard was right, it was very hard not to like him, despite the way he made her feel inside. "I bet she believes you too."

"Of course. When you want to badly enough, you can believe most anything." She was back at the bench, and he casually took up the opposite end to help move it. "Aren't there things that you believe in, no matter how unlikely or impossible they might seem?"

"No. Not anymore."

"The totally disillusioned Ms. Miller, huh?" He was studying her when she straightened up to face him. She couldn't tell if he was feeling pity or disdain when he said, "That's a shame."

Either way she didn't like it.

"Why? Why is that a shame? People don't have to believe in fairy tales and superheroes. They don't have to pretend life is better than it really is. That there's some sort of magic involved. What's wrong with being realistic? Life is unfair and people are human. That's all there is to it."

He felt neither sympathy nor scorn, but he was curious. This wasn't a pathetic disturbed woman speaking, this was a woman in pain. Hurt and beaten. A strong woman clinging to negatives to survive because they were simple and true, and all she had left.

"What about dreams?" he asked, betting himself that she had none left.

"What about them?"

"Aren't dreams food to the human spirit? Don't people need dreams, as unrealistic as they might be sometimes, to keep them moving forward? To give their life meaning?"

"Why do they have to be dreams? Can't they simply be goals you set for yourself? Can't they be realistic, one-step-at-a-time goals? Dreams are too easy to blow out of proportion. It's crazy to believe in things that may or may not be real, things that can't be, can't happen."

"Crazy or painful?"

She opened her mouth to answer then closed it. He knew. Two days, and already he knew she was a failure, a disappointment. Well, so what? She'd tried to warn him.

"Yes. Crazy and painful," she said, turning away to finish picking up. Unfortunately, there was nothing left to pick up. But to turn around and face him again was an intolerable thought.

She could hear him coming up behind her and braced herself. Still she trembled, as if hit by lightning, when he touched her shoulders.

"What happened to you?" he asked softly, the tenderness in his voice bringing tears to press and sting against the backs of her eyes. "Who hurt you?"

He wanted to turn her around and hold her in his arms, but she was so tense under his hands, he knew it would be like holding a plank of wood. The tightness in his chest began to ache, making it hard to breathe.

"No one," she murmured, more than a little uncomfortable with the topic . . . and his proximity. She attempted to step away but was held fast at the shoulders, then turned, so he could see her face.

"Tell me," he whispered, his eyes black and bottomless in the porch light.

If he hadn't sounded so caring, been so gentle, she wouldn't have laughed, wouldn't have pushed his hands away so forcefully.

"Look, I appreciate the help with the table, but it doesn't entitle you to butt into my life. Why don't you go turn something to gold and leave me alone?"

She took steps to walk away from him, but he snagged her left wrist and held tight.

"I can't," he said. "God knows I should. You're mean and you're nasty and . . . I can't. I don't want to leave you alone."

Had she thought him strange? He was just plain nuts. Couldn't he see she was trying to save him from the curse of her life? Didn't he know he was better off if her life didn't touch his?

"I'll hurt you," she said, explaining as best she could.

"Go ahead. Take your best shot. I'm not leaving."

She shook her head. He didn't understand.

"No. I mean I'll *really* hurt you." He frowned in confusion at her seriousness and slackened his hold on her wrist. She stepped away from him. "Stay if you want to, Scotty. I'm going inside. I'm doing you a favor, believe me."

Okay. The best he could do was give her a high score for originality and watch as she walked into the house and closed the door.

She was doing him a favor by not opening up to him? *She* was afraid of hurting him, not the other way around? Well, that was one for the books. Reverse rejection?

The porch light didn't go out until he was through the gate, which meant she was still watching him. But when he turned, the house was dark and he couldn't tell from where.

"I'm not afraid of you. You hear me, Ms. Miller?" he bellowed into the darkness, his voice echoing through the quiet neighborhood. "You don't scare me. I'll be coming back."

FOUR

He gave her Monday to reflect on and reconsider her hasty decision to ignore him, to think about him and anxiously anticipate his next move. He gave her Monday to miss him—and because he wasn't sure what he'd do next until Monday evening.

Growing up, it had been a joke at his house when his father would reject the title of Principal Hammond in favor of Mr. Jack-of-All-Trades. "It's not a part-time job," he used to say. "People call me Principal Hammond whether I'm at the school or not."

Of course, that hadn't meant much to Scotty until he was older, until he was old enough and wise enough to see that being principal was his father's vocation, not just his occupation. It didn't start and stop at the doors of the institution he was associated with. It was who he was, whether he was passing out diplomas at graduation or filling in nights for a sick janitor.

Scotty liked the idea of being *someone* and belonging to *something*. Being a son, a brother, a husband, a father, and belonging to a family. Being a teacher or a principal and belonging to a school. Being a good citizen and belonging to a community. It was fundamental and solid, safe and simple. There was no confusion in being who you were.

And so, when he'd accepted the position of principal at Tylerville High School he knew exactly what he was getting into. He knew how important high school was to a child's intellectual, physical, and emotional development. He knew small-town schools had small budgets, staff shortages, and limited outside resources. He knew it was up to him to maintain academic excellence, to promote community interest and involvement, and to provide the best possible experience for the students.

"I discovered almost immediately the loss of several intramural sports teams, the incorporation of the school newspaper into the English department curriculum, and that the drama club, debate team, chorus, and—for all intents and purposes—the entire art department had been cut away entirely by Mr. Kingsley to meet his budget. In essence, a lot of the fun stuff is gone," he told an eager, if a bit wary, group of his peers during their first preseason team meeting on Tuesday morning. Faculty meetings were a necessary evil they endured, to present and maintain a united front to the opposing team, their students.

The wariness that morning stemmed, no doubt, from the fact that he had been a lively player on the opposing team less than twenty years earlier and had scored more than once on many of his present teammates.

"Believe me," he said, sounding very grown-up in his own disbelieving ears. "I understand budgets. And cuts like these are necessary to maintain the core of the curriculum. However, we all know that not every student's talents will lay within the realm of the three R's. Isn't that right, Mrs. Fiske?"

Mrs. Fiske, the English teacher at Tylerville High since the dawn of time, arched a brow and said, "Once upon a time, I had not the slightest hope for you in that direction, Mr. Scotty Hammond." She paused. "Obviously, appearances can be deceiving."

He laughed and she smiled at him fondly.

"Time will tell on that one, I suppose, but being a late bloomer myself, I have a special fondness for kids who have to check out all their options before they settle on a career. And I believe it's our duty to expose *all* our students to as many adventures as they can handle. To give them every opportunity we can muster to try new things. To provide a safe testing ground for their youthful whims and dreams."

He gave that a few seconds to sink in, and when he saw heads begin to nod in tentative agreement, he continued.

"I've been mulling over an idea that I'd like your opinions on," he said humbly, knowing full well he could institute his idea without their opinions. "I haven't quite figured out what to do about the sports we've cut, but I've been thinking of starting a new tradition here at Tylerville High School." A pregnant pause. "A senior class play."

The silence that followed his announcement was ominous. Small towns were notoriously reluctant to change, and this included teachers in small-town schools.

"I know that in the past, the drama club put on a yearly presentation. This would be basically the same thing, except it would be extracurricular and the seniors would be responsible for it. And any profits they made would go to a senior class campout in the spring."

"A senior class campout? In the woods? All night? Together? With boys and girls together?" they asked, in a garble of exclamations.

He laughed quietly and went on. "The whole school could help with the play, for maximum exposure. This would give them a chance to experience acting, to sing if we do a musical. Art work on props, stage work, costuming, promotion, public speaking . . . a little bit of everything that was cut from the curriculum."

"But together? All night?"

"Just the seniors, with chaperons. And with their parents' permission. All of them months short of going to college and being off on their own anyway."

As he'd suspected, there was more resistance to the students' sleeping together than to putting on a play. When he made it clear that he'd be coordinating the project and that the campout could just as easily be a day at an amusement park, the friction shriveled

to a feeble rub. Deciding to do the play and leaving
the other matter up in the air—for further discussion
at a later time—brought their meeting to a rapid close
and left him with plenty of time to set step two into
motion.

The teachers' conference room at Tylerville Elementary School was as warm and stuffy two weeks
before the new school year as it had been two weeks
before the end of the last—a short eleven weeks earlier.

It had been a short summer for Gus. Finally being
able to afford some changes in her little house had
been so exciting in June. By the end of July, her energy was lagging but things were shaping up. The
house was beginning to take on a personality of its
own—warm, cheerful, comforting—and it was rubbing off on her.

She'd wake to sunshine soaking into and shining
off the muted yellow of her bedroom walls; she'd
stretch lazily, secure in her sense of belonging, and
reflect on the fact that she was truly happy.

Had she ever actually *known* she was happy before? She must have, because she hadn't always been
completely miserable, but . . . well, maybe she'd just
been too busy to notice it before.

Taking the time to notice your happiness sounded
ridiculous, but—

"Why, Scotty! Mr. Hammond," stammered the
principal, her dry droning of the school board's objec-

tions to the present health insurance policy ending abruptly when he sneaked, bold and noisy, into the room.

Gus's heart rate slipped automatically into panic overdrive. A vacuum sucked the air from the room and the temperature soared.

Like everyone else she turned her head to look at the interruption. A cool breeze in tan slacks, his white cotton shirt open at the neck, sleeves rolled up to his elbows—he tickled goose bumps across her warm flesh. His smile was as refreshing and exhilarating as a dip in a mountain lake. God, he was annoying.

"Mrs. Pennyfeather. Please, don't let me interrupt," he said, trying his best to appear repentant. Ha! Gus almost laughed. "We . . . we've had a bit of a brainstorm over at the high school this morning and I wanted to come over and get your input—since it would involve some of your students as well. But I guess it can wait till you're done here."

"Oh," she said, startled, confused, and curious. "Well, we were just finishing up. I must say, I can't imagine what all this is about. Did you want to speak in private?"

It was then that he looked about at the gathering, as if he'd just suddenly realized what he'd walked in on. His open, friendly gaze barely grazed Gus, still she felt targeted and pierced through and through. The fool winked at her.

"No no. No need for privacy. We were so excited about it at our meeting that it'll be all over town before lunchtime," he said, walking to the front of the room. He beamed that smile of his like a beacon in a dense fog, from one side of the room to the other, pulling every eye in his direction. "I confess, I was completely blown over by my staff's enthusiasm. A spark of an idea, and it caught on like wildfire."

"Well, don't keep us in suspense," Beverly Johns, the perky first-grade teacher, said. She giggled like a six-year-old and stared up at him adoringly. "Scotty, you're terrible to tease us like this."

Gus rolled her eyes toward heaven and prayed for strength. Well, she wasn't going to get sucked into whatever he was up to. No way. She wouldn't even look at him, she decided, tracing a heat circle in the veneer of the big wooden table with her right index finger, her left hand under the table rotating round and round and round—then back in the opposite direction.

"You always were fun to tease, Bev," he said.

She glanced up, caught off guard by the affectionate tone in his voice. He was grinning at Beverly as he slipped his hands halfway into his pockets. He looked very much at ease—as he did everywhere—and Gus wanted to loathe him for it. He quickly explained the situation at the high school and the plan devised to temporarily fill the need. Gus tried not to hear him, but he had a nice voice. Deep and low, infectious and entrancing, it had a tendency to vibrate with whatever emotion he happened to be feeling. It was a voice that was hard to ignore. Harder to forget.

Her thoughts strayed to that night, dark and intimate, mysterious and magical. Him, standing close and concerned, his hands on her shoulders, warm and gentle. His scent in her nostrils. Her heart racing. His words, "What happened to you? Who hurt you?" rang in her ears.

How would you tell someone like Scott Hammond—Mr. Damn Midas Man—that not everyone had the gift of turning everything they touched to gold? That the touch of some people turned things to dust? That it didn't matter if, in the wee hours of the night, his warmth and concern might have been a comfort to her soul, the risk of reaching out to him was too great?

How would you tell someone like Scott Hammond that some people were simply meant to be alone? That they hadn't the vaguest idea how to keep a man content and satisfied? That the future wasn't something they looked forward to? That it frightened them? That they couldn't be trusted with someone else's hopes and dreams?

Draw him a picture? Pencil a failure graph along her life line? Tell him the truth?

". . . working closely with your music director."

Gus looked up to find him staring down at her, his dark eyes twinkling happily. She frowned in confusion. "What?"

"Well, we did consider *A Midsummer Night's Dream*, but when *The Wizard of Oz* came up, it just seemed like the best vehicle for our purpose. Singing, dancing, acting, plenty of scenery and costumes . . . and with the addition of Munchkins, a bigger mandatory audience."

He chuckled with everyone else who knew that no mother, father, grandparent, uncle, aunt, cousin, or neighbor would miss the chance to see their favorite first- or second-grader dressed up as a Munchkin. At the same time, he studied her.

"Of course, if you think this is too big a project for you to handle along with your other responsibilities here at the school," he said, a calculating light coming to his eyes. "Well, I'm sure we could come up with a less challenging project for our first attempt at a senior class play. We'd probably also lose a lot of the enthusiasm and the momentum required to get something like this firmly rooted in the community, but . . ." He shrugged helplessly.

Slowly, she turned her head and then her eyes to the left to find everyone watching her expectantly. As this was only her second school year among them, she was still something of a newcomer, and an oddity, considering her background. She could see the uncertainty and hope in their expressions.

"I think I can manage to teach the children the songs," she said finally, refusing to look his way again.

Well, she intended to refuse, but was unable to help herself when he spoke again.

"Thank you, Ms. Miller," he said. "I was hoping I could count on you."

He wasn't teasing her. Their eyes met, exchanged suspicion and appreciation, then finally settled somewhere near the understanding that ultimately they were benefiting the children of Tylerville.

Of course, his first priority had to be the children. And it was. Truly. But that didn't mean it had to be to the exclusion of his own desires, did it?

No, he decided firmly, hammering in the last of the shingles he'd gotten to patch the hole in the roof directly above Chloe's bedroom. He'd left the elementary school feeling galvanized with energy. Not a common experience in the heat of the summer. He felt it would be best to tackle this project before he wasted the sensation on other things—like day-dreaming or a long nap in the shade—and before it rained again and ruined the newly painted ceiling below.

With no effort at all he could think of a million reasons to engage Ms. Miller in a little tête-à-tête, using the play as his best excuse. The possibilities were endless. *He* was a genius. And if he was careful, very careful, he could draw her out a little. Make her laugh. Trick her somehow into talking to him, *really* talking to him. And maybe, if he was careful, just maybe he'd get close enough to touch her again.

He laid the hammer sideways along the steep pitch of the roof to consider the prospects, to let his imagination run with them, then noticed another patch of rotten shingles over the eave a few feet away.

"Damn. What I need is a new roof," he said aloud, scooting closer to the edge. The house was old and the angle of the roof was sharp and treacherous. He'd used his last shingle, and a return trip back down to fix this new hole wasn't on his agenda. The top of a two-story building was not a place he'd choose to be if indeed he'd had a choice. However, if he didn't actually stand up, and if he kept his eyes focused on the shingles, it was almost tolerable. "What I *really* need is to win the lottery and buy a new house. Right, Bert?"

Bert lay on a shady spot in the grass below and barely quivered an eyebrow at the notion. The man was a dreamer.

Inadvertently, Scotty glanced down at Ms. Miller's roof, the gray-black shingles neat and orderly. He chuckled. There was a sparrow's nest in the gutter, he noted with a smile. She'll be wanting that removed when the leaves start to fall and the rainy season begins, he calculated, reaching blindly for the hammer.

He reached a little farther and a little farther until he finally had to look for it.

He leaned slightly to touch it with the tips of his fingers, to inch it toward him. He almost had it when the heavy end met gravity and slipped downward, parallel with the pitch of the roof. For the briefest of seconds it lay there, then he watched as it slid slowly down each row of shingles and dropped into his own rain gutter.

With a sigh and a weary stream of expletives, he rolled over onto his back, defeated. He looked into the thick, leafy canopy above him. Shade and bright sunshine crossed his vision in a rhythmic pattern as the wind rustled gently through the treetops. He was no handyman, he lamented, content to stay as he was a few minutes longer and ponder nature's beauty.

He could feel the warm shingles at his back through his shirt. He folded his arms behind his head and closed his eyes. It wasn't so bad on the roof.

And Ms. Miller had the sweetest mouth he'd ever seen—a shapely top with a chubby lower lip that he could spend the rest of his life sucking and nibbling on. He lowered one leg and left the other bent.

She'd kept her head bent low that morning, away from him, and the nape of her neck had almost driven him insane, he recalled with a chuckle. When he finally got his hands on her—and he knew he would eventually—he'd never voluntarily let go. Someone would have to pry them apart. He sighed deeply and crossed one leg over the other.

"Awwww," he screamed, sliding toward the edge of the roof like a log in a chute, his legs flailing in his attempts to prop his feet flat beneath him to stop himself. He heard leaves swooshing, limbs cracking, and incoherent gibbering as his life flashed before his eyes and death—if not a lifetime of excruciating pain in full body cast—rushed to meet him.

Panting and whimpering, he slowly came to the realization that everything had come to a stop. Time. Movement. His heart. It quivered in his chest uncomfortably, thumped out a beat, then another. When he had enough blood in his head to think straight, he gradually raised it to look down at his feet. The heels of his soft-soled shoes were wedged against the rim of

the rain gutter . . . his backyard sprawled porten-
tously miles below.

His head fell back against the roof. He sucked in
long, deep breaths, and, when he could, he looked
again to see how far away the ladder was.

Too far, he saw almost immediately. Squinting, he
could see the ladder had fallen away from the house to
rest in the branches of the old oak tree. In his fearless
youth it had been part of his escape route from his
bedroom window—now it seemed to have mature
limbs no bigger around than number 2 lead pencils.

Again, his head fell to the roof with a thudding
noise, and angry frustration churned in his belly. Was
the principal of Tylerville High School allowed to
cry? Then more constructively, he wondered if breaking through the roof into the attic was feasible. Did
he dare lift his heels from the gutter? Or should he try
to roll over onto his stomach?

That's when he heard the car pulling into the
drive between the two houses. He sighed heavily and
closed his eyes. It would be too much to hope that it
would be one of his sisters. The car door opened and
closed. He had to make a quick decision.

Gus was exhausted. She'd forgotten how tiring being "on" for other people could get for someone with
a solitary nature. Raised in a strict, regimented envi-
ronment, she was more of a social caterpillar—slow,
prickly, eager to cocoon herself—than a friendly but-
terfly like Lydia.

She was hot too. The August heat was humid and
cloying, she could feel the air passing in and out of

her lungs as she breathed. A cool shower and some uninterrupted, air-conditioned "down" time would put her day in perspective.

She got out of her car and slammed the door. That idiot neighbor of hers had ruined her whole day. She glared at his house as she walked up the drive. If he was sincere about this business with the senior class play, all right. But did he have to confuse the issue with winks and innuendo? Did he have to make her skin tingle with the idea that he had ulterior motives in involving her?

"Ms. Miller?" came a croaky whisper. Scotty cleared his throat. "Ms. Miller?"

No response.

"Ms. Miller? Is that you?" Nothing. "If you're not Ms. Miller, but you can hear me, please answer. I need help," he said as calmly and with as much dignity as he could muster. He listened but heard nothing but the birds in the old oak tree. "Hello? Is anyone there?"

She stood still and slowly scanned the area. She frowned, narrowed her eyes, and scanned it again.

Finally, he heard footsteps on the concrete drive.

"Hello? Mary? Beth? Elaine? Chrissy?" he called, listing his sisters first, and then, as a last resort, adding, "Ms. Miller?"

"What are you up to now?" she asked, the irritation in her voice causing him to cringe. "If this is another one of your stupid tricks to get my attention . . ."

"No. No."

". . . I'll tell you right now it's not going to work."

"No. Wait. Please."

"I cannot *bee-lieve* the people of this town hired someone like you to set a good example for their children. You're more of a child than all of them put together, I swear. Where are you?"

"Never mind," he muttered softly, closing his eyes. "Just let me die here."

"I mean it, Scotty Hammond. We're going to have this out here and now. Show yourself or I'm going inside."

"I can't."

"What do you mean, you can't? Come out this instant. I want to know what all that business was at school this morning. Is nothing sacred to you? I've had time to think about it, and if you dreamed this whole scheme up just to get to me, you should be ashamed of yourself."

He was taking his life in his hands, he knew, but there was a principle involved here. He wasn't *totally* devious.

"That's pretty bigheaded of you, don't you think?" he called to her. "It just so happens that the idea for the senior class play came to me long before I ever saw you. I admit, I was leaning heavily toward *A Midsummer Night's Dream*, but all things considered, *The Wizard of Oz* is a much better idea."

Your involvement notwithstanding, he failed to add.

"Then why did you wink at me this morning? You

did that on purpose, just so I'd think you were up to something, didn't you? Just to annoy me."

He wondered how long it would be before buzzards found him.

"Yes. I did it to annoy you. I *enjoy* annoying you."

"Where the hell are you?"

He hesitated. "I don't think I want you to know anymore. I'm beginning to like it here."

"What?"

"I'm on the roof."

"What?"

He took a deep breath then clipped out each word, clear and concise. "I'm on the roof of my house. I was patching a leak. I've lost my ladder."

"You've what?"

He thought a moment, then decided he'd rather swallow shredded glass than repeat himself. He folded his arms stubbornly across his chest and listened as the squeaky gate to his backyard opened and closed.

Bert barked once. He'd intended it as a gracious greeting, but he could see the woman took it as an intruder alert. For the life of him, he couldn't figure out why the woman was so afraid of him. He always wore his best, most friendly face when she was around. Still, some humans were a little more stand-offish than others—so it fell to him to bridge the gap. Perhaps she'd enjoy a good joke today, he thought, standing and pointing to the man with his nose.

Gus approached the giant dog slowly, only half-sure he wouldn't eat her. She kept turning her head to get a good look at the roof, but could see nothing until she was standing next to Bert.

"Oh my," she said, laughter gurgling in her throat but not crossing her lips. Bert heard it and knew he deserved a reward for making her happy. He slipped his big head under her hand and scratched an itchy spot on his left hip by rubbing it against her leg.

Scotty raised his head to scowl down at her. His heart twisted and sank in his chest. She was completely beautiful. Standing there in the shade of the old oak, a sunbeam filtering through the leaves to dance light in her dark hair, to sparkle in her eyes. She was smiling, happier than he'd ever dreamed of seeing her. So incredibly beautiful, she took his breath away.

"Oh my? That's all you're going to say?" he asked, knowing that despite his elevation he didn't look as lofty as he sounded.

"No. I'm sure I have more to say. Just give me a second."

"You know," he said solemnly, cherishing the sight of her. "It would be very unkind of you to enjoy this too much."

"Would it? I don't think so," she said, crossing her arms in front of her and shifting her weight to get comfortable. "I think this is one of those once-in-a-lifetime opportunities. I think I should slow down, smell a few roses, savor the moment."

"All right," he muttered, resting back on the roof to ease the strain on his neck. He knew women better than he knew metric conversion tables. He wouldn't be leaving his present position till she was good and ready to let him.

Bert laid down on the woman's foot—a clear indication that he was glad she'd decided to stay awhile. She was a quiet, undemanding soul, and he liked her.

"What's holding you up there?" she asked.

Addressing the sky, he explained about the gutter and how he'd come to be perched on it—and when no immediate reply was forthcoming, he lifted his head again to catch her pulling a lawn chair into the shade and sitting down, crossing her long legs, and arranging the skirt of her dress.

"Comfy?"

She smiled up at him. "Yes, thank you. You?"

He grimaced. "What do you want?"

"Want? Why, nothing. Can I get you something?"

He wasn't so humiliated that he couldn't see the humor in the situation—knew he'd behave in the exact same way if their situations were reversed—but he was also getting a little vexed. He wasn't used to being in this position—not his position on the roof and certainly not in the position of being someone's joke of the day.

He restated his question. "What do I have to do to get you to push the ladder back against the house?"

Her top leg began to swing in a trifling fashion, and she smiled. "Golly. Don't you just hate it when you have an infinite number of choices? I mean, choosing from five or six or even a dozen things isn't bad, but when the options are unlimited, it's so confusing. Don't you think?"

Something deep in his heart started to make him wish he hadn't thrown the trash in her yard, that he hadn't teased her in church or disturbed her violin lessons or . . .

"So maybe you should narrow my field of selections to what you're *willing* to do to get me to push the ladder back against the house."

Hmmm . . . what wasn't he willing to do?

"I know you don't have too many scruples," she went on, "and that you'd stoop pretty low to get what you want, but where exactly do you draw the line?" Just in case the negotiations went on into the night, he bent one leg, worked to get a solid footing, and started to push himself higher up the roof. "That's an interesting question, isn't it? How far would Scott Hammond go to get what he wants?"

Almost a foot from the gutter, he wasn't quite ready to roll over and sit up, so he raised his head and looked down at her. "I'll always go as far as I have to, if what I want is important to me. What's wrong with that?"

Gus couldn't answer. There was nothing wrong with that. Not so long ago she might have answered the same way—when some things were still important to her.

"So, what's important to you, Scott Hammond?" She was curious. "What is it you want?"

A personal question at last. She was showing an

interest in him. This was good. This was a call to sit up and think carefully.

He gathered his thoughts and spoke when he was ready.

"People are important to me. The people I love, even people I haven't met yet. Who I am and what I do stems from their influence on me." He paused. "I want . . . a full life. Nothing out of the ordinary, nothing grandiose, just a job with purpose, meaning, something that's worthwhile, worth doing. And people to love, to share with, to care for." Keeping his knees bent, he leaned back on his arms. "I'm not a brilliant man who'll discover the cure for some disease. I'm not an ambitious man. I'm not even a very handy man," he said, motioning with his head at the patched roof. "I'm just a man with good intentions. I like to be happy. I like seeing other people happy. I'm a simple man. So what I want and what's important to me are simple things."

A purpose in life and people to love? That's all he wanted? All that was important to him? That's all? That was all she wanted, all she'd ever wanted. So what happened? What went wrong? What was he doing so right that she was doing so wrong? *Everyone* loved Scotty Hammond. *Everything* he touched turned to gold. What was his secret? Or were some people just naturally more lovable and prone to success than others?

Whatever the innate difference was between them, she couldn't help but resent him a little . . . and envy him more than she could ever say. What really got to her was the way he spoke of his good fortune. He was lucky and he knew it, content, delighted even, with what he had.

"What about you, Ms. Miller?" he asked. She could feel him watching her. "What's important to you? What is it you want?"

"I don't remember," she said, getting to her feet. Keeping him captive on the roof wasn't much fun anymore. He was clearly the better person, and she couldn't maintain her superiority any longer—circumstantial though it was.

"You don't remember? Or you just don't want to tell me?" he asked, sitting up, watching her walk slowly over to the ladder.

"There's nothing to tell."

She grunted, using all her strength to push the tall extension ladder vertical to the house, then one inch beyond, till it fell back on its own.

"Then tell me about those scars on your wrist," he said, making no attempt at the ladder. He watched her, waiting to see if she'd answer.

She looked at the scars on her left wrist, fingered them gently, then smiled and looked up at him.

"They really bug you, don't they?"

"How they got there bugs me."

"You're going to be disappointed," she warned him.

"Try me."

She took a deep breath and let it out slowly. He was clearly fascinated with the scars, and she was about to remove all their mystery and make them

mundane. Well, he'd get used to these little disillu-
sionments about her.

"Three years ago, almost four now, I guess," she
said, examining her wrist and what had once been a
more defined Z-shaped scar traversing it. "I had surgery here. Nothing tragic. Nothing serious. Just a
routine operation to release the pressure on the nerve
running through it."

"Pressure from what?" he asked, scooting toward
the ladder while she was busy talking.

"The tendons in there. Carpal tunnel syndrome
they call it. The tendons get inflamed and start to
swell, put pressure on the nerve, usually from some
prolonged repetitive motion."

"Like playing a violin?"

He was starting down the ladder. She moved to
hold it steady for him.

"Yes, exactly."

"And what happens after a surgery like that? Obviously, you can still play the violin."

"Yes." She swallowed hard, stepping back from
the ladder when he was relatively safe. "After a rest
period and some anti-inflammatory drug therapy and
wrist splints and classes on stress-reducing movement
techniques and a lot of exercise. You can still play the
violin."

He stepped off the last rung and turned to her. He
took her wrist in the palm of his hand, looked at it,
then into her eyes, searching.

"But . . ."

Her hand and arm were sizzling from the heat of

his. She felt small and weak before him, her failure so plain to see in her eyes.

"But you can't seem to play as well as you did before," she said, then cleared away the frailty she heard in her voice. "Or practice as long. Or convince anyone that just a little more time and a lot more work will restore your talent to the near perfection it once was."

For a long moment he watched unshed tears shimmer in her eyes. He was on the verge of gathering her close, to hold her near, to absorb her pain. But she blinked and lowered her eyes away from him. Gently, almost reluctantly, she pulled her hand from his. He started to take it back but stopped, knowing his chance was lost.

"I'm sorry to disappoint you," she said after an awkward moment passed between them. "I know you were hoping for something a little more exciting, a failed romance maybe or a . . . ah . . ."

"I'm not disappointed," he said softly, wondering what she'd do if he kissed her. "And the only thing I was hoping for was that whatever it was, it didn't hurt anymore."

All right, enough was enough. If he was going to be kind to her and sympathize with her and understand her heartache, she was going to have to leave.

"It doesn't," she said, twisting her wrist around and around in the air for him. "See? Good as new." She wasn't fooling him. He knew her pain was fresh and raw and far from healed. For half a second she thought he might even suspect that her truest pain had nothing to do with her ability to play the violin. "And now that you're safely on the ground, I think I should go."

"But I didn't give you anything."

"Give me anything?"

"For pushing the ladder over. For saving my life. You never told me what you wanted. Or what I had to do."

"Oh. Forget it," she said, in a sudden hurry to be away. Why did he always have to stand so close to her? Couldn't he say what he had to say from the other side of the yard?

"Forget it? No way. I always pay my debts and I'm extremely indebted to you."

She knew where this was going. Knew he'd never give up the bone she'd inadvertently thrown to him.

"Yes. Yes, you are, come to think of it. But I need more time to think of a proper payment."

"All right." He wanted more time with her but would have to settle for a promise of another meeting. He could sense that she'd laid a great portion of herself out in front of him, and that she was feeling exposed and vulnerable, that she'd run hard and fast if he tried to hold on to her too tight.

So, he'd let her go—for now—and try to decipher just exactly what it was that she'd revealed to him. More than the surgery, more than its lasting impact on her skills as a violinist. There was more to what she'd told him than the sad, sad facts.

Then again, he thought, watching her ease away from him. She fully expected him to let her leave without a protest. And wouldn't it be a shame to be so predictable?

"Ms. Miller," he said when she turned to go. "Now that you've saved my life, and since my dog likes you so well," he nodded at the proud escort showing her the way to the gate, "don't you think it's time I called you Augusta?" He stepped in front of her. "Or maybe Gus?"

He said Gus as if it were spelled s-e-x. Soft and low, like a whisper in the dark. His dark eyes were warm, bottomless, consuming. His gaze lowered to her mouth and came back to her eyes in a blink. Was he thinking of kissing her? No, that couldn't happen. Well, it could, but she wouldn't like it. Well, she'd probably like it but it wouldn't be good. Well yes, it probably would be good but she wouldn't be happy about it. Well, maybe she would be . . .

"Um, sure. Augusta would be fine, I guess."

Without touching her, he leaned forward and barely brushed his lips against hers with his eyes open. She didn't twitch a muscle, didn't dare. And then he did it again! A slow, thin coating of tingles washed over her. The last thing she saw was his eyes closing, slow and euphoric, as if he had a piece of heaven in his mouth. His lips pressed against hers, opened slightly, and he traced the seam of her lips with his tongue until they opened.

She lost track of what happened after that. . . . The breeze died, the birds went silent, her world reeled. Her hands were fifty-pound weights on the ends of her arms. Her feet took root in the grass. In her belly a quiet riot took place—a coup—as long-suppressed emotions took over the established numbness.

Scott's hands turned to fists as he fought the urge to crush her in his arms. If he didn't stop while he had half a clear thought in his head, there would be no stopping.

He watched her eyes open, dazed and unseeing at first, murky green whirlpools of passion and confusion. She was startled—by her own behavior more than his—and this enchanted him.

He smiled. "A token of my gratitude," he said, referring to the kiss.

A vague nod. "Or Gus. You could probably call me Gus too. Either one. Whatever." A nervous laugh escaped her. "Just not Gussie," she said, backing away. "My grandma used to call me Gussie. She died. Well, not because she called me that." She laughed. "I hated it, but I wouldn't . . . But when she did die . . . No one else calls me Gussie." She turned, opened the gate, slipped through and closed it in one quick maneuver. "I've always been sort of grateful for that. I just don't think I *look* like a Gussie."

There was some muttering on the other side of the fence and then he heard her screen door close. He touched his lips with two fingers, amazed that he could still feel her there, warm and soft and sweet as a peach. He grinned at Bert.

"*That*, my friend, is what dreams are made of," he said, tugging fondly on one of the dog's ears.

FIVE

Bertrum T. Goodfellow missed the young one. Not at first, of course. At first it had been something of a relief to get away from her. But lately, he'd noticed he was almost glad to see her coming.

Since he and the man had moved into the big house, she hadn't once flung herself across his back and insisted on riding him. And the fascination she'd had with pulling his lip up over his nose to get a good look at his teeth seemed to be a thing of the past as well.

Nowadays, she rode around on wheels. On occasion, she and the man wrestled together on the living room rug, laughing and shrieking—until the man played dead or the young one ran off quickly to the bathroom. Sometimes they'd sit close and read, or play a game with a ball and a stick in the front yard. Today they were coloring the walls in a room on the second floor.

He'd gone up to check on them several times—but even if he hadn't he would have known they were up to something messy. They usually were.

Three quarters of the way through his forty winks he was aroused by the distinctively light and rapid cadence of the young one's footsteps. Because it was his job when the man wasn't around, he followed her and found her covered head to toe with red paint in the backyard.

For a little while it looked as if she were trying to paint the fence with the front of her clothes. He didn't want to know why. But as he grew weary of watching her and started to lay down in the shade, she toted a lawn chair over to the fence and opened the gate to the woman's habitat.

They both liked the woman's habitat. So bright and neat and cheerful. He thought the flowers smelled heavenly, and sniffed appreciatively as the young one picked them, roots and all. It wasn't until she trotted over to the screen door and let herself in that Bert got worried—and only then because the woman had made no provisions for four-legged visitors.

Gus thought she heard her back door open and close, but it happened so quickly and unexpectedly that she wasn't entirely sure she'd heard it at all. No sound followed, so she continued to practice. Bruch's G minor concerto had the greater part of her sense and concentration, the tips of her fingers sliding against the fingerboard, the music humming in the strings of her violin. It was a deeply romantic piece she hadn't played for several years. It somehow appealed to the confusion in her soul.

This was *his* fault, too, she thought, drawing and sliding the bow with more verve. This confusion. No matter how often she straightened the things about her—the pictures on the walls, the books on the shelves, the stacks of music, pillows on the couch— she still felt unsettled. Discontent. Itchy as poison ivy.

She'd searched high and low for music that was unfamiliar to her, music she had to focus on to play, music that would wipe out the memory of the kiss she'd shared with *that man*. Why had she allowed that to happen? Curiosity? If so, the knowing didn't make living next door to him one bit easier.

It was fast becoming a bad habit, to have to stop playing and shake off the excited chills spreading across her shoulders and down her arms, in order to clear her mind of everything but Bruch.

"Did you goof?"

Gus jumped, then stood there staring at a little girl. At least, it looked like a little girl. Where a partial coat of bright red paint permitted, she could see short dark hair and big brown eyes with long thick lashes, a heart-shaped mouth, and a blue T-shirt with "Daddy's Little Girl" written on the front.

"Who are you?"

"I'm Chloe. You goofed, didn't you?" she asked, nodding with a sympathetic expression on her face. "I could tell."

"You could?" she asked, recovering slowly, but enough to walk across to the living room window to look for the child's father, who, no doubt, had orchestrated this intrusion. "Do you know that music? Have you heard it before?"

She thought it unlikely considering her father's taste in music, but it couldn't hurt to ask.

"No. But when you goof it hurts my ears." She put one hand flat over one ear and a fist full of root flowers over the other. "It's like someone is screaming."

Gus nodded her understanding, and with no father in sight, directed herself to the next important issue.

"Those are pretty flowers. Where'd you get them?"

"I picked 'em for you," she said, holding them out to her, shaking clumps of dirt onto the spotless hardwood floor. "If you put them in water they won't die."

"Thank you," she said, unable to be angry with a face as innocent as the daisies she took in hand. "Would you like to know another trick with flowers?"

"What?"

"Well," she said, leading the way back to the kitchen by following the path of dirt on the floor. "If you *pick* the flowers, instead of pulling them up, they'll come back next year. Then you can pick them all over again. Come on, I'll show you."

"All you do is play music all day?" Chloe asked, following close on her heels.

"No. I teach music too."

"My daddy's a teacher."

"Yes, I know." The girl was on her tiptoes, peering into the sink at the flowers.

"Are you dry?"

"Yep," she said, running her little red hands down the front of her shirt and holding them up to show no paint had rubbed off—as if Gus could tell. "This is an old shirt anyhow. Daddy made me wear it, 'case we ruined it with paint."

She leaned over to scratch an itch on her knobby little knee and, Gus noted, left no new paint on it.

"Good idea. What are you painting?" she asked, opening a drawer and removing her kitchen scissors. She took one of the small jelly jars she kept for her nephews to drink from out of the cupboard. "That's a very pretty red."

"I know. I picked it myself. Daddy said I could cuz it's my new bedroom and I can paint it any color I want. Except black. And not the ceiling. He already painted that. It's white. Oh-oh," she said when they heard a pathetic whining noise at the door. "There's Bert. He wants to come in too."

"Ah—no," she said hastily as Chloe started for the door. "Let me just show you how to cut these flowers and then you can go back out and play with him. Okay?"

As simply as she could, she explained to the attentive Chloe that the roots needed to be left in the ground. "And if you forget to bring scissors with you, you can hold the stem here and here and break it off, see? And they'll still live awhile in water."

"I'm not allowed to play with scissors like yours.

They're too pointy and I'll poke my eye out. I have some that I can use, but they don't even cut paper very good."

"Oh. Well. I guess you'll have to break the flowers off then, and be sure to leave the roots in the ground. It's easy to do it that way too."

"Are you going to play more music? Can I listen? I can hear it at my house, but I can hear it better here."

"What about your daddy? Does he know you're here?"

As if on cue, Bert let loose a bloodcurdling howl that had Gus's knees buckling, and at the same time they heard Scott calling for Chloe.

They met at the back door.

"Chloe," he said, an exaggerated frown clouding his handsome and usually jovial expression. "What have I told you about leaving the yard without permission?"

"I can't," she said, unabashed and unafraid of her father's scowling countenance. "But if you open the gate, then it's just one big backyard instead of two little ones," she added brightly.

"No," he said, shaking his head and entering Gus's kitchen to get closer to his child. "The gate stays locked unless you have permission to open it. The other yard belongs to Ms. Miller. You have to have permission from Ms. Miller to go into her yard and you have to have permission from me to leave ours. Understand?"

"Permission. Permission. Permission. All I ever do is get permission."

He put his hands on his knees and bent low, in to her face.

"I'm sorry, but that's the way it is, kid. Everybody has rules they have to live by, remember? Some are to keep us safe. Some are just to help us remember to be polite to other people. We all have them, and you have yours, and you know there are consequences for breaking them."

Chloe had a most wonderful frown. Her brows drew together in waves and looked like a little black caterpillar slinking across her forehead. Gus loved it. To see it pointed fearlessly at its adult version was very amusing. A soft laugh escaped her and both frowns turned her way.

"Do you have so many rules, too, Ms. Miller?" the girl asked.

"Oh yes," she said, nodding vigorously. "Different rules. Big-people, adult rules. But yes, lots of rules."

"Can I have a drink?" she asked. Scotty opened his mouth to tell her it was rude to ask for things at someone else's house, but Gus stopped him with a hand.

"Sure. Juice okay?"

"What kind? I like apple best."

"What luck. I have apple."

When she moved away from the counter she'd been leaning against, Scotty saw the jelly-jar vase full of daisies, stood up straight to look out the kitchen window, then met her gaze with a doomed expression.

Gus would cherish that look till the day she died. He was mortified.

"Chloe," he said, his voice filled with a dissatisfaction that caused an instantaneous knee-jerk reaction in Gus. "You didn't pick Ms. Miller's flowers, did you?"

"She sure did. Aren't they pretty?" Gus said, cutting in before Chloe could understand that she'd done something wrong—despite her good intentions. "She got a couple roots with them this time, but we went over that and she'll be more careful next time. Right, Chloe?"

"Right," she said, smiling as she took the juice and swallowed it down in three or four big gulps.

Scotty was watching her, his eyes keen and searching, but he said nothing. Instead he waited for Chloe to finish her drink, reminded her to say thank you, and told her it was time to go home.

"But I wanna listen to the music," she said.

"You can listen to it from our house."

Hmmm. . . . When Scott Hammond put on his father hat he was like a totally different person. Gus was fascinated. If *that man*, Scott Hammond, had had a foot in her door—not to mention his entire body— he'd have been combing the rugs for every feeble excuse he could find to stay and pester her. Principal Scott Hammond would have done the same thing in a smooth, relaxed businesslike fashion. But Daddy Scott

Hammond seemed almost eager to leave, she noticed, watching him herd Chloe toward the door.

"Tell you what, Chloe," she said when it was becoming clear that a revolt was imminent. "I'll give you time to get home and find a comfortable chair or maybe a bed to lay down on, I'll open my windows wide, and I'll play a piece just for you. How's that?"

"A piece of what?" she asked, unwilling to consider the proposal without all the information.

"A piece of music. I know a song about a girl who painted her bedroom red, but she was much, much younger than you. She was five."

"I'm five!"

"Are you? I would have sworn you were . . . six, maybe seven."

"No. I'm five."

"Well, the girl in the song is five too. Would you like me to play it for you?"

"Yes," she said, eager. "But don't play a piece of it. Play the whole thing. Okay?"

"Of course. And you know, this is the kind of music that doesn't have words. You have to close your eyes and relax and picture the girl in your head. Think you can do that?"

"Sure, I can. I can do lots of things in my head. Come on, Daddy."

Daddy didn't run off right away. He couldn't take his eyes off Gus, who looked up and was immediately tangled in his web of enchantment and desire. He hadn't forgotten about their kiss either. She could see it in his eyes—the heat, the passion, the memory of it.

His lower lip slid between his teeth as if he could taste her there, feel her.

Her heart was pounding high in her throat, blood swooshed in her ears; she felt a little dizzy and her fingers were numb. She knew she was breathing—hyperventilating really. Her mouth was dry.

"Should I, um, wait? Long enough for you to clean her up?" A soft, nervous laugh. "She's a mess."

Silently he shook his head, then he finally said, "Three more hours and it'll be bath time. An hour after that is bedtime. I'll be out on my front porch by nine."

It wasn't as if she could respond with a "that's nice" or a "goody for you," because he wasn't merely imparting the information, he was inviting her to join him, daring her to meet him there, tempting her to be with him.

He was gone before she could give him a specific answer, one way or the other. But with time to think, she settled on the other. Already she was more involved with Scott Hammond than she wanted to be. He was like a brain fungus. Anything more would be cruel and self-destructive. No, the best thing she could possibly do for both of them would be to avoid him like . . . like unscooped poop on a sidewalk. She should walk around him, jump over him, cross to the other side of the street if she had to.

Of course, if when eight forty-five rolls around and a person's left wrist is aching from too much practicing that day and there's nothing on television and she's already read the same page of her book three times without comprehension and she's longing for a breath of fresh, warm summer-evening air— well, what harm could come from stepping out on her own front porch for a moment or two?

She left the light off and was careful not to let the screen door slam. Rather than sit in one of the freshly painted wicker chairs with their bright kerchief pillows, where she might be easily seen, she lowered herself down on the top step and leaned against the wrought-iron railing.

The first time she saw her house, it had been a quiet summer evening much like this one. As often as she thought about it, she'd never been too sure if she'd fallen in love with the neighborhood or the house first. Both were such throwbacks to a time that was, in her mind, innocent and peaceful. A time when it was okay simply to be, without being *someone*. A time when rolling in the grass was encouraged, when twilight was magic and not a menace, when your neighborhood was as big as the world would ever get.

Had her life ever been that uncomplicated? Or were the memories of her early childhood really just dreams? When had roller skating on the sidewalk in front of the house been outlawed? When had violin practice taken precedence over swinging from the trees?

She loved this neighborhood. She loved that the men mowed the lawns on Saturday morning. She loved watching the children on their bikes and the impromptu ball games in the street. She loved her role as fussy old Ms. Miller, whose job it was to fetch their balls and skateboards from her flower beds and appear put out. She loved listening to the mothers calling suppertime, and the quiet when everyone was safe and sound in their beds.

She loved the idea that her neighborhood was only one of billions just like it, that people all over the world were doing the same insanely routine and infinitely normal things she could remember doing before her life slipped between the jaws of a vise. Mankind had gone on without her, but it hadn't changed so much that she couldn't find a place to fit in again. Nor had she been squeezed and molded into something it couldn't embrace again, come to think of it.

Strange, that hadn't occurred to her before—that maybe her music hadn't changed her as much as she'd thought, that living differently didn't necessarily make you different inside.

Truth be told, she hadn't really done much thinking lately, just reacting. Everything seemed to happen so fast. The pain. The surgery. The looks. The pity. It all seemed like part of the swirling blue water in the toilet bowl, that disappeared along with her career in a matter of seconds. Then there was Tylerville and the children, and only now did her life feel calm enough for thought. For replanning, rebuilding . . .

Nearby, a screen door bumped closed softly. She cringed and scrunched herself a whole size smaller.

What was she doing? Reacting again. Cowering instinctively in the face of change.

Obviously she'd wanted to be there, wanted Scott Hammond to know she'd met his challenge, that she wasn't afraid of him and that she wanted to be with him. Knowing he was on his front porch waiting for her had her blood sizzling with excitement, her nerves jittering with anticipation. She wanted him, she realized with an exhausted sigh. She did. Had, all along.

She lowered her head to her hands and rocked it slowly back and forth. She couldn't fight him and herself.

The sound of his footsteps in the gravel drive had her jumping up. She did the Indecision Shuffle on the top step. Hide? Go inside? Stay?

He yelped when she sprang up before him at the bottom of her front steps.

"You scared me," he said, his hands automatically reaching out to her.

"Sorry." She shied away from his touch. It made pins and needles in her feet and fingertips.

"It's okay," he said with a soft laugh, moving his hands to his chest for lack of a better place to put them. "I didn't think . . . I thought . . ." He started to laugh.

She wanted to laugh, too, but was afraid it would come out sounding a bit hysterical.

"Hi," he said, starting over.

"Hi."

"I'd invite you to walk but I want to be able to hear Chloe. How about a swing?"

A swing?

"Oh. On your porch . . . Sure."

"She's a pretty good sleeper normally," he said, groping in the dark for her. They were between streetlights and visibility was poor. He was afraid he'd walk into her, knock her down. "But it's still a new house and a strange town with different night noises."

"I understand."

He used her voice to pinpoint her and finally just reached out and took her arm. She startled.

"I'd have left the porch light on but . . . bugs, you know."

"Oh, me too," she said self-consciously, acutely aware of his light grasp. "I mean, that's why I left mine off. The bugs. Too bad the moon isn't full."

The gravel crunched loud under their feet as they both realized a full moon would have been *very* romantic, and while romance was certainly in the air, the most significant emotion on their plate at the moment was an unmanageable awkwardness.

"Careful," he said. "Chloe's bike is here somewhere."

"I saw the two of you earlier," she said, picking her steps painstakingly. "You'll be taking those training wheels off soon, she's almost got it."

"Maybe. She and her mother live in a condo, so she doesn't get much chance to practice. And she forgets between visits with me."

"Well, they say that once you learn, you never forget how." She felt a slight tug on her arm and followed his lead to the porch, rattling on, "Liddy can still ride a bike. Before Todd came along, she and Alan used to take the other two boys for long rides in those little seats? On the back of the bikes? They had little helmets for them and everything."

"Did you learn to ride?"

"No time," she said, walking up the steps beside him. "I had to practice."

He suspected there were many childhood activities she'd missed out on and that a listing of them would depress them both. He led her across the porch and offered her the swing, but didn't sit down next to her.

"Can I ask you something?"

"Sure."

"Your flowers this afternoon? We had a little talk about picking other people's flowers, Chloe and I. I'm sorry I didn't say something to her earlier. I didn't anticipate that she'd—"

"Oh. I wish you hadn't." She had to move. She couldn't just sit there while he stood looking down at her. "I mean, I'm glad you did, but I wish you hadn't. She . . . Her intentions were good."

"Her intentions were good?"

"Well, she picked them for me. To please me. I just didn't . . . wouldn't want her to think I was disappointed or unhappy with her gift."

She'd moved to the railing and was looking out at the lights glowing softly in windows up and down the block. Shamefacedly, he admitted silently that he would have automatically reprimanded Chloe there on the spot, embarrassed her and spoiled her gift, if he hadn't been stopped. She was pretty astute for a woman who had no children, he thought. Then again, maybe not having children made her more sensitive toward them.

"I owe you twice then," he said, sensing he'd be running up his debt to her at a steady pace. She glanced over her shoulder, askance. "First the ladder, now the flowers."

She laughed softly and turned back to the night.

"She liked the music you played for her," he said, moving to sit on the rail beside her. "She said it sounded happy."

She smiled. " 'Fiddle Head Reel' it's called. I liked it when I was a little girl too. My father played it for me." A pause. "I haven't come across many songs about little girls who paint their rooms red, I'm afraid. Think she'll mind, if she ever finds out?"

He chuckled softly. "No, not at all," he said. Silence wedged between them, like an unwanted third person. They both struggled with it, but Scotty was first to elbow it out of the way. "What was he like? Your father."

"Quiet." She shrugged and walked a few feet away to the top of the steps. Seconds ticked by before she added, "He never called himself a violinist. He would either say he played a violin or a fiddle, but he wouldn't say he was a musician. He was self-taught. He played by ear but couldn't read music, and there was some sort of distinction there for him. He played with a band, in Irish pubs mostly, sometimes Western bars. He played it all—jazz to sixties folk music."

"But he wasn't as good as you," he assumed.

She turned to him and leaned against the big white pillar holding the roof up, shaking her head gently. "No. In many ways he was much better. I love the music and I respect my talent. He did, too, but he also loved the instrument. The violin. In my heart I think I could have just as easily picked up a flute or sat down at a piano, learned to play and loved the music just as well. For him, it was only the violin. The sound, the shape, the feel of it in his hands. His face would light up every time he picked it up, and he . . ." she hesitated, ". . . he went somewhere else when he was playing it. Heaven, maybe. You could see it in his expression and the way he moved and . . ." She laughed softly. "Sorry. That's probably more than you really wanted to know."

"No. I like people stories. They fascinate me. I'm a people person, remember?"

"You've no doubt noticed that I'm not, ah . . . a people person."

"No. I hadn't noticed that. People here like you, kids adore you. I hadn't noticed." He tipped his head to one side, curious. "So, what sort of person are you?"

It was a perfect night, clear and quiet. So clear the stars looked like diamonds spread out on black velvet, there for the taking. So quiet they didn't have to raise their voices to be heard. She sighed.

"I'm not sure anymore."

"All right, then, what sort of person *were* you?"

"Not a very deep one, I guess," she said sadly.

"Otherwise, I might have been better prepared when my life turned upside down."

"Prepared for what?"

"I don't know. The rest of my life, I guess."

There it was again, that lost and confused quality about her that was so at odds with the plucky, independent woman she personified. He crossed his arms over his chest to keep from reaching out to her, holding her near, then giving her a good shake to make her see what she had, what she'd accomplished, who she was to the people who cared about her. Like him.

"What is it that you think you want from the rest of your life?" he asked, hoping there was room for him in it. "I asked you before and you said you weren't sure anymore."

"I'm not. I just . . ." she said, then she went quiet for a long moment before she finished. She had to tell him the way things were for her. He needed to know. "I just don't want to hurt or disappoint anyone ever again."

He shut his mouth and tried not to stare so hard at her dark profile, it was making his eyes water.

"And who have you hurt or disappointed so far?" She might not appreciate his prying, but he couldn't stop himself.

"The who hasn't been list is shorter," she said with a derisive snort. She walked slowly to the pillar on the other side of the steps, distancing herself on every level. She leaned back against it and spoke softly, half hoping he wouldn't be able to hear her, and wouldn't care enough to ask her to repeat it. "That's what I do, Scotty. I disappoint people. I hurt them. I don't mean to, but I do it. Regularly. I somehow convince people to invest their wisdom and expertise, their love and their hopes and huge portions of their lives in me, and then I let them down."

He couldn't stand it any longer. Approaching her slowly, he reached out and put a hand on both sides of her face, angling her head into what little light there was to see it.

"I tried to warn you," she said, hoping he could at least see her sincerity. "I'm not good with people. I put on a good show but . . . but the people closest to me always . . ." He was going to kiss her. He was strumming her cheeks with his thumbs. Her skin prickled and tickled back to her ears and down her neck, across her shoulders. "I'll disappoint you too. Eventually. I will."

"How could you possibly disappoint anyone? You're talented. You're smart. Beautiful. You're sweet and compassionate when you want to be. You're funny. Clever. Strong. I don't understand."

"Please don't touch me," she said, ducking out of his reach, her heart beating so hard it ached. "I'm trying to explain so you will understand. I . . ." She took a deep breath. "Every teacher I ever had thought I could be a world-class violinist, that I had something special. For hours, months, years they worked with me. Day after day," she said, holding her hands out to show the vastness of the time involved. "They taught me everything they knew. They sacrificed their time and energy for me, and I was never . . . I was never anything but good. Not great. Not phenomenal. I frustrated the hell out of them," she said, her voice going low and flat with her own defeat. "Every time one of them would finally admit that there was nothing more they could teach me, they'd pass me on to someone else, thinking they'd let me down somehow. Disappointed that they weren't the one with the key to open up that special something in me. My father got out early, knowing what it would be like. But my mother never gave up. She hired an agent and a publicist." She put both hands behind her. "But I wasn't a ten-year-old savant or a legendary virtuoso. I was just a really good violinist. Really good and really ordinary. She had to settle for Carnegie Hall and first chair with the Philharmonic. And I worked my butt off to keep it because—surprise, surprise—I wasn't the only really good violinist in town."

"But that's nothing to spit at. That alone is an accomplishment very few—"

"No no. Stay away. I want to finish. It gets better," she said, staying just out of his reach. "See, after a couple of years I gained some respect with my peers. I was one of the youngest people ever to join the orchestra. I was never late, never missed a rehearsal or a performance. I worked hard, I wasn't temperamental. After a while some of the pressure eased away, and I found five minutes to fall in love with this really cool saxophone player, Nelson Forge, who believed in freedom of expression and taught me that being a classical snob was beneath me. He showed me how to have fun with my violin and explore different types of music. We were on tour in Europe and he took me to all sorts of little pubs and taverns where saxophones and violins made totally different kinds of music than what I was used to . . ." she hesitated, ". . . made my father's kind of music, actually. Everything was so romantic. My first trip to Europe. My first love affair."

He didn't like that she'd gone suddenly silent thinking of this saxophone player, didn't like it at all.

"What happened?"

"We came home. My five minutes were up. The tour was over. Europe was gone. I tried to keep up with him. I really did. But we were out most nights, all night, and my wrist was starting to hurt. . . . It was September already and our season lasted from October to May—until August if you include the stadium concerts. I couldn't . . . I was a huge disappointment to him." A short, harsh laugh. "I played with the pain in my wrist for as long as I could, until the slightest movement made me want to cry." This was the hard part, the part that involved him. She had to tell him she couldn't satisfy a man, he needed to know. She took a deep breath and blurted it out. "And let's face it, you sometimes have to move around when you're having . . . you know, an affair. I . . . I couldn't keep him happy, I couldn't satisfy him, I couldn't . . . I . . . I caught him with another woman." She went silent, waiting for the vivid

mental pictures, the heartache, the tears to over-
whelm her. But they didn't. She felt nothing, and she
sighed with relief.

"I wasn't even surprised," she said when he made
no comment. "Hurt, but not surprised. It was just
part of the pattern. He wasn't the first person I'd
failed, and as I was soon to find out, he wasn't going
to be the last." She hesitated. "My mother wept the
morning I had surgery. I heard her. She told the doctor my whole life story and cried when he told her
that with some effort I'd eventually play as well as I
ever did."

Scotty was astounded by her thinking. He felt
crushed inside, not by her story, but by the weight of
the guilt she'd inflicted upon herself. He didn't know
where to begin. From the beginning, he supposed,
when she first took on the responsibility of fulfilling
other people's dreams and wishes instead of her own.

"The rest you know," she said quietly, the tone of
her voice as empty as her jar of self-worth. She walked
to the railing, keeping her back to him. "I've told you
all this to save us both a lot of time and pain. Obviously, we're . . . attracted to each other."

"Obviously," he said, able to agree with her at
last.

"If we don't act on our impulses, these feelings
will eventually go away."

"Gus," he said, undaunted.

"I don't want to hurt you, Scotty. I think I could
fall in love with you, but knowing that I'd hurt you,
too, is . . ."

"Augusta."

"So, you see, it's really much wiser not to start anything that's doomed from the beginning."

"Ms. Augusta Miller," he said, loud enough to get her to turn around.

"What?"

"Come here."

SIX

Scott Hammond was such a stupid man. An idiot. A fool.

Hadn't she just told him what a mistake it would be to get involved with her? Hadn't she just explained why she didn't want to get involved with him? Hadn't he heard a word she'd said?

The darkness between them was thick with desire—hers as well as his. But if he wasn't going to listen to reason, then it fell to her to save them.

"Come here," he said again, his voice low and soft, sure and alluring.

"Scotty . . ."

"Come."

She swallowed hard and took a step forward. It was easy.

"This is a huge mistake."

"A little closer."

"We're going to regret this." Once started, she

took step after step. She had no will to stop herself. She didn't *want* to stop.

"Closer."

She could actually feel it when she broke into his personal space. It was warmer and charged with excitement, undercurrents of passion and consuming greed. She felt a hand on her waist, pulling her nearer. He palmed her cheek, his fingers at the back of her neck drawing her toward him.

"You're a very stupid man," she said with her last normal breath, before the air caught in her throat, behind her heart.

"Don't you believe it," he said, taking a firm hold about her waist, breathing in the sweet scent of her, enjoying the warm, soft texture of her skin. "I'm a lot of things, but stupid isn't one of them."

He skimmed his mouth over hers, teasing, coaxing. Defying fate. She started melting away like the Wicked Witch of the West.

"This is so wrong," she murmured, trembling as she brushed her lips against his.

"Then why does it feel so good?" He kissed her. "So right?"

Good question. But she'd have to think about it later, when the earth wasn't spinning so fast and her senses weren't screaming to touch him, to taste him, to feel him.

No, he wasn't a stupid man. He drugged her hard and fast with long, deep kisses, depressing her thought processes, stimulating her nervous system, transporting her to a world where only he was real and only she could touch him. He got high as the feel of her, soft and firm, smooth and curvy, coursed through him, filled him, devoured him. He hungered for her. Got lost in the tiny impotent noises she made, in her unsteady breathing, in the fluttering of her heart beneath her breast.

He kissed like a French whore's tutor. Hot, deep, devouring. Then slow, erotic, demolishing. His hands fisted in the folds of her skirt, bunching the material, exposing a long shaft of shapely leg and softly round buttock. His skin was so warm through the thin cotton of his shirt. Her fingers were frantic to get at it. He pressed her pelvis tight against his, bent over her to touch the soft, smooth skin of her inner thigh from behind. He turned her abruptly, to prop her weakening weight against the house. His hand tangled itself in her panties, pulling the fine, silky material snug against her throbbing desire. The pressure was an excruciating delight.

A muffled cry in her throat had him moaning with his own need. He'd found a whole new world in her mouth and didn't want to leave, despite his temptations to wander far and wide into other unknown territories. God knew he wanted to, needed to, but he kept coming back to her mouth like a kid to a candy store, never pacified, unable to secure it all in one visit, enraptured by the endless diversity.

Weak and barely able to stand, she was suddenly aware of being led gently by the hand, across the porch to the door. If more kissing was all he had in mind, the darkness would have provided them plenty of privacy. If he needed to sit down, there was always the swing. . . .

"Oh my," she said.

He responded with a light chuckle and opened the screen door, passing her in before him. Arguing with her would be useless, he knew. Her mind was made up. She was a failure, a disappointment. It would be quicker and easier—and a lot more fun—to spend the rest of his life showing her how special she was.

It never occurred to her to tell him she didn't want to go inside with him. It would have been a lie, and the way she was behaving, he wouldn't have believed her anyway. They were destined to ruin, and she couldn't remember being happier, or more optimistic. Or less afraid.

"What about Chloe?" she whispered, feebly grasping at straws as his arms snaked about her from behind, his mouth sipping at her throat below her ear.

"She's upstairs sound asleep." His hands made quick work of the first few buttons on the front of her dress and then his mouth moved to her shoulder.

"What if she wakes up?"

"She won't."

"But what if she does? What'll you do?"

He turned her around to face him. He held her face in his hands, kissed her tenderly, then said, "If she wakes up, I'll go to her. I'll give her a glass of water and tell her a story. I'll wait for her to fall back to sleep. What'll you do?"

She smiled and gave him the only answer that came to mind.

"I'll wait for you."

There was not one inch of her that didn't feel as if it had been touched by something magical, something mysterious and powerful that could come back at any moment and seize her again. Carry her off. Devastate her world.

She could hear birds chirping and feel the heat of the sun on her face, but if she opened her eyes, the dream she'd had the night before would be over.

She was warm and comfortable. Her body was weighty and sluggish with satisfaction, her muscles aching sweetly when she stretched.

"Don't move." The words came in two firm syllables from the man beside her. She managed to lay perfectly still for several seconds before she started to laugh. He groaned and rolled, looping one arm across her chest. He nuzzled and cuddled, muttering, "Go back to sleep."

Turning her head toward him on the pillow, she found him half-awake, his eyes warm and affectionate, still clouded with the passion of their lovemaking.

"I think I should go," she whispered, touching her nose to his playfully. "Chloe'll be awake soon."

"She'll watch cartoons till eight. You can leave then." He pulled her close and closed his eyes.

"She'll see me then."

His eyes opened and narrowed to study hers. "We're going to have a *secret* love affair?"

"Don't you think we should? At first? For a while? To make sure it works?"

He grinned. "I gotta tell ya. It's working great for me."

She laughed softly and Eskimo kissed him again. "Me too."

"Then why worry?"

"I just don't want to get everyone's hopes up, and then disappoint them later if it doesn't work out between us."

He pulled away to get a clearer look at her face. "Are *you* hoping it works out?"

Taken aback, she wondered if he thought she'd be in bed with him for any other reason.

"Actually, I am," she said softly, hesitating only a moment before she exposed her heart's desire.

He gave her a quick reassuring kiss. "Me too. I'm dying to see you as one of those tall, bony, super-proper old women with your mouth all puckered up in disapproval, scolding me for carrying my teeth around in my shirt pocket at our youngest son's wedding and . . ."

"With my mouth all . . . Our what?"

"Son. Our youngest son." He raised up on one elbow to look down at her. "I should probably tell you now that I want sons. As many as you'll give me. I'm in dire need of male companionship."

"You want them right away?"

"As soon as you can arrange it."

"You couldn't just join a baseball team for this male companionship?"

He curled one leg over both of hers and lowered his head to her breast. Her heart beat steady and strong. He'd gotten the answer he wanted. He'd seen it in her eyes—that strange soft glow that women get when they think of babies. She wanted one.

"It's not the same," he said, making a huge to-do of sticking his arm under the covers to touch her soft, warm belly. "I need someone who doesn't already know how to stand in front of a toilet or how to shave. Who doesn't already know the significance of over-time or the distance between home base and the pitcher's mound. Someone who doesn't already know how great duct tape is. I want someone I can teach all that stuff to."

She was grinning. "And you can't very well teach Chloe how to make those disgusting noises with your armpits, can you?"

"Well, no. I guess I shouldn't have," he said, and when she started to laugh, he wrapped his arms around her. Cradling her head in his hands, support-ing himself with his elbows, he said, "So you see my problem?"

"I do. You have a very serious problem."

"I know. And I'm very serious about it," he said—though he didn't really need to when the amused sparkle in his eyes died away to reveal the somber thoughtfulness behind it. "So, tell me this. With my hopes as high as they are, and with you actually hop-ing things work out between us, who do you think will be more disappointed if they don't? You and me? Or everybody else?"

It seemed as if he was trying to make a point; she just wasn't sure what it was.

"Us, of course. I only meant that we should consider Chloe and my mother and—"

He kissed her to silence her.

"I know what you meant and you're probably right about Chloe. She's already learned the lesson about grown-ups not getting along sometimes, and we probably shouldn't rush it. The two of you have just met, you need time to get used to each other," he said, his gaze lowering to her mouth, her chin, her neck, her chest. She was so beautiful to him. Then he looked up suddenly. "But beyond that, beyond the three of us, it doesn't matter what anyone feels or thinks about us being together or not. We're the ones with the most at stake here. We're the ones who'll pay the price. And . . ." he said, laying a finger against her lips when they opened. "And we'll pay it in equal portions. Understand? You won't hurt less than I do or be happier than I am. Our dreams are equally important here. Okay?"

She agreed, but she didn't really understand. He brushed his lips against hers. Playful and enticing. But maybe it was him who didn't understand. What did he know about disappointment, anyway? The Midas Man. Who had he ever disappointed? She hadn't even begun to disappoint him—and yet . . .

"Tell me about your wife," she said. "Can you tell me what happened?"

He raised his head slowly to look at her. "Now?"

She knew the look in his eyes, felt his arousal against her thigh, and started to laugh. "If you wouldn't mind, in fifty words or less?"

He chuckled, shifted his weight a bit, then frowned in concentration.

"Nothing really *happened*," he said, looking back on it. "It wasn't as if we cheated on each other or fought a lot. We were young when we married and our life was complicated—with Chloe coming a little sooner than we'd planned, working, and both of us with school to finish. I was substitute teaching and working on my master's degree, and Janis was just finishing up her MBA and planning to go on to law school. But we were happy then. I finished up and got a full-time job. Janis started law school a semester late after having Chloe, but she made it up the next summer. There was a day-care program at the high school I taught at, and I'd take Chloe there sometimes, so Janis could study. If we had a problem, there always seemed to be some way to work it out. The crazier our life was, the happier we were—the more we needed each other, depended on each other, and valued the other."

"So, what happened?" she asked when he seemed stumped on the memory.

He shook his head. "Life got easier, I guess. I was cutting my teeth as principal of a big inner-city high school, and she was a promising young clerk at a big law firm, Chloe was just three and starting preschool. We could finally afford to take a short vacation. We left the baby with Jan's mother and went to the Bahamas for five days. On the fourth morning we woke up in each other's arms and . . . just sort of stared at each other." He frowned, remembering. "We were two people in bed together with nothing in common, no common goals, wanting different things out of life. We cared about each other, but we weren't in love anymore. It wasn't anyone's fault. What we had just fizzled away."

"That's it? No blowout? Nothing?"

He rolled away onto his side, no longer in the mood, and propped his head up in the palm of his hand.

"No. We tried to make it work. We stayed together a little longer. For Chloe. For ourselves. Saw a couple different marriage counselors, her mother's minister . . . It just wasn't there anymore."

"So you ended it."

"Basically," he said, nodding, his eyes clear and steady on hers. No anger. No regrets. No doubts. "She came home from work one night and said she thought we should—she thought she might be falling in love with someone else." She cringed in sympathy at that, and he grinned. "By then I'd been looking at other women for a while." He shrugged. "It was only a matter of time before one of us said it."

"And was she, is she, in love with someone else?"

"The jury's still out, but yeah, I think so. Maybe. She quit her job, rearranged all our lives, and moved all the way to Springfield to be with him. I'd say she was feeling something for him." He laughed and reached up to play with a stray lock of her thick, dark hair that wasn't spread out with the rest in a long tangle of curls across her pillow. "You know, if I were more philosophical about life, I'd be tempted to say that my marriage turned out the way it was meant to."

"You would? Why?"

He traced the ridge across her lower lip with his thumb and wasn't at all surprised to feel his desire for her stir once more.

"Because now I have the job I've always wanted. I'm living in a house I don't have to pay for. And I've met you."

She smiled, quickening hard and fast, her insides twisting into a greedy knot of need. She reached up and caressed his stubbled face, thoroughly amazed that she could. And because she could, she lifted her head off the pillow and kissed him.

No great philosopher, she didn't care how they came to be together, only that they had. The new-found awareness of her own happiness had struck her with force and intensity, and she wasn't about to question it. Enjoy it. Relish it. She'd cling to it as long as she could. A week. A month. A year—if good luck really existed.

He put his palm flat on her chest and pushed the pale blue sheet down her body, below her navel. A cool breeze sent chills across her skin. His hot mouth dropped to her breast. Exquisite pleasure swelled up in her, gurgled in her throat. Her back arched, and she squelched a flicker of guilt at her selfishness. She *wanted* this. She *wanted* to be happy. She wanted to love and be loved—if only for a while. Happiness was her right, and God knew, she was due some.

She rolled toward him, slipping her leg between his, pressing close to him when his lips met hers, clever and eager to please her. He leaned back, pulling her with him until she was on top of him. Kneading her firm buttocks, he let her feather kisses about his head and neck indiscriminately.

The world came to a screeching halt—and so did they. Their eyes traveled upward toward the ceiling where they heard Bert's toenails tapping across the floor above to greet Chloe into a new day.

"Oh dear," she said, suddenly standing beside the bed, tugging the last remaining tucked-in corner of the sheet loose to wrap it around her nakedness. "Quick. I have to go." In a fluster, she was gathering her shoes and dress and underthings and holding the sheet and leaving and wanting to stay all at once. "Did I bring my purse? No. God, I don't think I even closed my front door."

He couldn't help laughing. She reminded him of a nearsighted bird come in through a window, bouncing off the walls in an effort to find her way out again. Reaching for his pants, he thought he should help her before she knocked herself out cold.

"Oh sure, you laugh now. Just wait till you have to explain this to her," she whispered loudly. "I don't have time to get dressed. I'm taking your sheet. I'll bring it back later."

"Bring it back for breakfast."

She gasped, surprised by what a great idea that was. She laughed softly.

"This is insane."

Passing her on the way to the door, he planted a kiss on her mouth, saying, "Completely insane. And you're loving it." She grinned, unable to deny it as she tiptoed past him into the hall. He grabbed her arm, spinning her around toward the back of the house. "You laugh now, but just wait till you have to explain this to all the neighbors."

She giggled. Clandestine love affairs and sneaking home in a bedsheet were new to her—and truth to tell, she was loving it. She'd bet her hair was a mess, too, but she didn't care. Who would have thought the quiet, seemly, regimented Augusta Miller would ever feel so brassy, wanton, and careless?

He opened the back door for her, followed her out onto the porch, and held the screen door for her. Then because he wasn't ready for her to leave him—and because her hands were full of clothes and bedding, he walked with her to the gate.

She hesitated before going through, made a vague gesture toward his house, and finally stepped forward to place her hand, palm flat, on his bare chest.

"Thank you," she said, sensing it was a silly thing to say. Yet what more could you say to someone who'd rescued you from a prison, who'd mixed hope into the unrest of your heart, who'd awakened you with a kiss as if he were a prince in a fairy tale?

He grinned, dimples denting his cheeks deeply,

fully aware of her meaning. "Hurry back and I'll scramble your eggs too."

She giggled. "And I thought you were obnoxious before. What have I done?"

He took a tender hold of her chin, tipped her mouth up to meet his. "You've made me very, very happy. That's what you've done." He kissed her again, his hands moving low on her body. "Think this bedsheet is big enough for both of us? Let me in."

"No. Stay away from me," she said, holding the sheet tight, backing herself through the gate, giddy with happiness. "Should I bring apple juice?"

His lecherous grin turned to a warmer, more meaningful smile. "She'd like that."

The look in his eyes had her feeling more self-conscious than if she'd been standing there naked. She wasn't used to being looked at as if *she* were a rare and precious gift—only the vessel of one. It was embarrassing. Recalling that Chloe liked apple juice was *not* that big a deal, but if it elicited that sort of response . . .

"Anything else? Milk? Cereal?"

He shook his head. "Just hurry back."

SEVEN

Gus always felt that September was wholly misunderstood. Generally considered to be one of the autumn months because of the distance of the sun from the equator, in its heart it was still part of summer, clinging desperately to early sunrises, warm days, and balmy nights well into October as proof.

School started, but her heart as well cleaved to the sensations of summer. Redolent, romantic, fraught with life. Certainly she'd never felt more alive, more passionate, more acutely aware of subtle changes in the air.

The children, too, were hanging on to summer like leeches, tapping its energy, bleeding its spirit of freedom dry.

"Behave now. Keep your hands to yourself or you'll have to sit on them until the bell rings," she said sternly.

"I don't wanna. And you can't make me."

She gasped at such impudence. "Guess again, pal. Just because I'm the music teacher, doesn't mean I don't have a ruler around here somewhere to rap your knuckles with."

"You can't do that. I'll sue you for assault."

"Oh yeah? Then I'll sue you for . . . for . . . mental cruelty."

"Mental cruelty?" he said, laughing as he continued to slide his hands up her bare thighs, her dress no obstacle at all. "You don't look as if you're suffering much."

"I will be if the children catch us like this," she said, unable to stop grinning. Scotty had her pinned against the blackboard in the music room, rendering *pianissimo* kisses over her face and throat, his hand movements clearly *agitato*. She squirmed to get away from him, and he grinned—*affectuoso*. "Is this how you behave at your school?"

"Who would I behave like this with? Mrs. Fiske?" he asked, chuckling at the picture in his mind, releasing her skirt—just in case.

"Carolann Goreman? I met her at the last school board meeting. I don't think teaching biology was a random decision for her."

"Me either, but . . ." he said, between tiny nips at her neck, ". . . she doesn't smell nearly as nice as you do."

Rubber-kneed and mentally foggy, it was several seconds before this registered.

"How would you know what she smells like?" she

asked, catching him in a comparable condition and twisting easily out of his grasp.

"Eau de formaldehyde?" He laughed and let her go, discretion being the better part of most things in life. Besides, it was almost as satisfying to see the rosy flush of her skin and the vivacity that seemed to have taken up a permanent residence in her eyes of late. Well, almost. "Poor Ms. Goreman's perfume turns a corner before she does."

"What a terrible thing to say," she said, pretending to be shocked as she prudently maneuvered so the piano was between them. "She wasn't overly fragrant when *I* met her."

A slow, smug grin settled into his expression. "You aren't jealous, are you?"

"Me? Of course not," she said, holding her head high even as she recalled how green and mean she'd felt the day she'd watched him with his sisters—and she'd barely known him then. "I trust you."

"Do you?" he asked, glad to hear it because he sometimes wondered about it.

"Sure," she said. And she did, but that didn't mean she wasn't constantly watching for signs of discontent in him. If the pattern of her life held true, he would love her and be faithful until she did or didn't do something to change his mind, until he discovered how ordinary and imperfect she really was.

"Then give me your panties."

"What?" She was instantly hot and shivering with chills despite the fact that she was pretty sure she'd heard him wrong.

"Your panties. Quick. Give them to me," he said as a bell rang in the hallway.

"No. Why? No. What for?" she asked, backing around behind the piano as he walked toward her, smiling like a friendly wolf.

"You trust me, don't you?"

"What's that got to do with my underpants?"

"Just give them to me. I want to carry them around in my pocket all day."

"No. That's silly."

"Please, Gus?" His voice was as soft as a kiss, his gaze as ardent as a lover's touch. Mesmerizing. "Take them off."

Anxious and confused, she worried her lower lip and tried to decode the look in his eyes, sensing it was more than a challenge or a dare. More than a simple act of trust. His request was like a sex act, as personal and intimate as making love, but scary and thrilling like doing it in an elevator.

"It'll be our secret," he said. "Something only the two of us know."

She swallowed and teetered on the edge of titillation.

"Gus," he whispered, soft and urgent. His gaze hot and pleading.

Breathing quick and shallow, her heart racing, her mind growing dull as excitement and desire curled low and deep inside her, she bent to lift the skirt of her dress. Her hands trembled when he leaned slightly over the piano to watch them. There was a boldness, an entirely feminine, erotic, and naughty

sensation that she couldn't contain as she lifted first
one sandaled foot and then the other, couldn't hide
when she rose to face him with her panties in hand.

"You keep looking at me that way, and sitting on
my hands will take on a whole new meaning," he said
soberly, until she laughed. He laughed with her, but it
only added spark and light to the fires of lust smolder-
ing in his eyes. "Now I know, for sure, that you'll be
thinking about me all day."

"I think about you constantly," she said, leaning
against the back of the piano to be closer to him, a
kiss-me-again smile in her eyes.

"No, I mean *really* thinking about me," he said,
meeting her halfway. "Touching you, kissing you, in
you . . ."

A movement in the window of the door caught her
attention—she hid her panties behind her as if the
piano were transparent.

Seeing the look on her face, he responded naturally, turning casually to face the door when it
opened. Beverly Johns held the door open for her
thirty-one first-grade students, and they filed in, smiling at Gus, eyeing Scotty with open curiosity.

"Good morning, Ms. Johns," he greeted her.
"How are you today?" he asked, blinding the woman
with his grin as he meandered around the piano,
passed behind Gus, snatched her panties, and stuffed
them into his right pants pocket. "Looks like you've
got a great group of kids here."

"I do," she said, all but batting her eyes at him.

"So far, I think this may be the best group of first-graders I've ever had."

This being the second week of school, it was understood by everyone over the age of reason that her statement remained to be seen for several more months yet, but that positive reinforcement and a little ego boost couldn't hurt the end result.

They exchanged a few more words, but Gus was too distracted to pay much attention. There was so much air and freedom under her skirt. Her thighs were tingling as if they'd never brushed together before. She'd worn a soft cotton half slip under the thin fabric of her dress, it was cool and smooth against her overexcited skin.

Somewhere in the back of her mind she was shocked and scandalized by her behavior. But up front and in her heart she felt like a vamp. Sexy and seductive. Full of sensual secrets.

Scotty, on the other hand, was growing uneasy. There were the panties in his pocket, of course, but at the moment it was the look on Gus's face that threatened to be his undoing. Standing perfectly still, her hands sedately clasped on the top of the short, boxy piano, her eyes were dreamy and glazed, and she was smiling like a cat with a live mouse in her mouth. If she'd gone to bed and started without him, he couldn't have felt more left out. She was turned on and ready, and he didn't dare cross the room to her.

He bandied a few words with Ms. Gray while her second-graders were finding places to sit on the floor, but his eyes kept gravitating toward Gus and the euphoric look on her face. With the addition of the two kindergarten classes, the music room was becoming crowded and noisy, and when he simply couldn't restrain himself any longer, he used the hubbub and confusion to do something about it.

Removing his sport jacket, he laid it over the top of the piano, very nonchalant, and joined her on the other side. He rolled up his right shirtsleeve and most of his left before leaning toward her and whispering, "Feel good?"

She nodded and smiled at one of the children waving to get her attention.

"Let's see," he said, even as his right hand slipped behind her to stroke her bottom, one cheek at a time through her dress. She continued to nod and smile at the children, he noticed, but her eyes grew larger and rounder with each stroke. "Mmm. Care to join me in the hall, Ms. Miller?"

She laughed out loud then and shook her head, appearing for all the world to see to be declining a juicy offer from the notorious Scotty Hammond and innocently moving away from him as if he were a sweet but pesky suitor.

"That boy will never change," Ms. Feldhour murmured under her breath as she walked away from her group of five-year-olds, alongside Gus. "I think he likes you, Augusta."

"We're neighbors," she said, hoping that would explain everything.

"Well, you play your cards right and you might have something there," she said, nodding sagely. "I'll never forget, I taught him in Sunday school years ago, and he was the sweetest little boy . . . and shy, if you can believe it."

"That is hard to believe," she said, glancing back over her shoulder at him, returning his conspirator's grin.

"Oh, not for an instant," she said, not wanting Gus to get the wrong idea. "He's still one of the nicest, sweetest young men I know. I'm so pleased that he's returned to us."

"Uh-huh," she said, fairly certain she'd never be able to convince anyone in Tylerville that Saint Scotty Hammond the Midas Man was walking around with her panties in his pocket—even with her bare butt as proof.

Not that she really minded. She sort of liked being with someone everyone liked. Someone every single woman in town wanted to be with—some of the married women, too, for that matter. It was empowering to think that of all the women he could choose from, he'd chosen her. She didn't fully understand it, mind you, knowing what he did about her, but for now . . . at that moment she was glad—head to toe—that he liked living dangerously.

"Boys and girls," she said, flicking the overhead lights off and on to get their attention. "It's time to use indoor voices and to find a place on the floor to sit. When the lights stop blinking it'll be time to sit quietly and pay attention."

This was also a cue to the other teachers that she

was ready to take over the class and for them to go take a break.

"We don't usually meet all together like this, do we?" she asked, addressing the large group of children aged five to seven, speaking loud enough to be heard over the last few children who were ignoring the bright lights. When they, too, had settled, she continued. "We have a special guest today. This is Mr. Hammond. He's the principal at the high school, and he's come here today with a special request."

Normally his introduction would have been followed by a perfunctory round of applause. But as the children were considerably less impressed by him than their own principal, Mrs. Pennyfeather, they merely turned to him with wide-open stares of interest.

"Ms. Miller," he said, sounding amazed. "You didn't tell me you had so many well-behaved students. I'm very impressed."

Gus and the children exchanged proud smiles, and Scotty didn't miss the genuine affection that went with them.

"Ms. Miller did tell me that you were some of the best singers she's ever heard. Is that right?" he asked, smiling at the confident confirmation he received.

With a small shake of her head, she watched Scotty wrap the children around his little finger. Charming little girls with his smiles, eliciting total devotion from the boys with man-to-man eye contact. Clearly he was a little-people person too. She envied him his social prowess. He always knew what everyone wanted. Respect. Appreciation. A joke. A little sympathy. A pat on the shoulder. A reprimand. Empathy. Hugs. When the time came, would he understand her as well? Or would his disappointment be too great for even him to get around?

She sighed and leaned back against the wall as he explained the play to the children. The wall was cool, and she unconsciously wedged her hands between her backside and the wall, then smiled. On the other hand, he might very well be the death of her long before she had an opportunity to disillusion him, she thought. And that wouldn't be so bad—being loved to death by Scotty Hammond. A girl could do worse.

He passed out permission slips to be taken home to their parents, thanked them all very sincerely for their attention, asked them to remind their teachers that the first organizational meeting would be held after school that day, and then turned to Gus with a singular look in his eye.

"You'll be there this afternoon, won't you, Ms. Miller?"

"Yes, of course, Mr. Hammond. I wouldn't miss it," she said, retrieving his jacket from the piano for him.

"And will you miss me?" he asked in a voice for her ears only.

"Every time I miss my underpants."

Which, as it happened, turned out to be nearly every second of the day. It was astonishing to realize just how often one backed into things, used a hip to open a door, perched oneself on the edge of a desk, or was patted in that general vicinity by a short person wanting one's attention.

Pantyless driving was a new experience as well, and air-conditioning added to the exhilaration of it. To say she was merely missing Scotty by four o'clock that afternoon would have been a gross understatement. She craved him. Needed him like air to breathe. Couldn't wait to get the meeting over with and get home to him. . . .

The high school was a long, low building, H-shaped with the offices, cafeteria, gymnasium, and auditorium in the connecting hallway. She was a few minutes early, but not so much so that she'd actually expected to see Scotty in his office when she passed by it on her way to the auditorium.

She was so distracted and eager to see him again, it was several seconds before the noises filtered into her mind. She stopped and looked about the empty hallway as the muffled clamoring reached her a second time, drawing her attention to a custodian's closet several paces behind her.

Paying it little heed, she continued down the hall until it occurred to her that the light was out and the door closed. Suspicious, she hesitated. The noises came again, rhythmic now as if someone inside the closet was attempting to draw attention. Soft, muted noises that carried barely ten or twelve feet, and with no one else around . . .

She approached the maintenance closet thinking an animal or a bird or perhaps the janitor himself was trapped inside, though why he hadn't turned the light on . . . maybe it was blown out.

She knocked first and called hello. No answer meant it was some sort of animal, a couple of lovesick teens perhaps, a thief, or a—

"Ah!" she yelped when the door suddenly opened and she was pulled inside.

"Shhhhhh . . . took you long enough. Shhshhshh," she heard Scotty's whisper in the dark, as she fought off the hands that seemed to be touching her everywhere at once, under her skirt.

"Scotty?" she hissed out, her heart beating so hard, she was trembling.

"Shhhhh. I've been waiting in here forever. What took you so long? I was going crazy," he said, backing her against the wall as his mouth sought hers. When they met he made the sounds of a starving man at an all-you-can-eat buffet, and she started to giggle.

"Scotty. The meeting," she said, gasping the words between hungry, deep kisses. She had his belt loosened and was working on the button at his waist.

"Remind me *never* to keep your panties in my pocket again," he murmured, his face at her neck, hands pushing the buttons on her dress at the speed of light. "I had to sit at my desk all afternoon. I skipped lunch. Jayne and Beesley took their damn sweet time leaving the office to go home. God, you feel good."

The keys and change in the pockets of his slacks clinked on the floor as he pushed the top of her dress off her shoulders, en route to the hooks on her bra. She worked her arms from the sleeves and went back to tugging on his boxers, going limp with pleasure when his mouth clamped down on her breast.

Like two minks in a sugar sack, they went at it. Pressing and caressing. Touching and tasting. Pushing and plunging. Feasting and fondling. With her skirt twisted high about her waist he cupped her, delighting in the heat and moisture as long as he could bear to before he stooped to lift her leg as high as his waist. She adored his unyielding desire a moment longer, then guided him gently toward hers, sucking in a whimper of extreme pleasure when he filled her, hot, hard, and deep.

They ruled the janitor's closet with passion and delight. No kingdom ever knew such happiness. No star such heights, no ocean such depths of emotion. In no other land would needs be met with such enthusiasm and ease, would contentment reign so freely and completely.

Panting hard and laughing softly, they clung to each other as their souls floated slowly back to the earth.

"Gus, I love you," he said when he could, using what energy he had left to hold her tight against him. He filled his mind with the sultry smell of her, the texture of her hair, the exact temperature and texture of her skin. Memorized them, because if nothing else, the long afternoon he'd spent thinking about her had also made him realize how much he needed to see her eyes light up with affection for him, to hear her laughter in his life, to feel her—solid and real—in his arms. "I love you, Gus."

"Oh, Scotty," she murmured, swallowing hard around the lump of emotion in her throat. "I love you too. I just . . ."

She wanted to tell him that whatever she did to hurt or disappoint him in the future, it wouldn't be intentional. If she could arrange it, the rest of his life would be a lark. He'd never be sad or worried or hurt again. He'd never be lonely or anxious or disappointed. If she could, she'd see to it that each day slipped into the next gently with love and tenderness. She'd fill his life with joy and excitement, and when he closed his eyes to sleep, his dreams would mirror the peace in his heart. If she could.

"You just what?" he asked, using the wall to push himself away from her.

"I just wish you knew how much."

Moving his hands to her face, he planted a tender kiss mid-forehead.

"You worry too much," he said, reaching for his pants. "You can't measure how much someone loves you, anyway, can you?"

Maybe not, she thought, straightening her own clothes. Maybe it would be easier to measure someone's patience and understanding or calculate just how much frustration and anger someone could tolerate. But then, if their love outweighed all other emotions, it would seem reasonable that the bulk of their forgiveness would increase as well. So, maybe measuring love wasn't so far-fetched.

"Besides, how many other men would you give your panties to?"

"None," she said, most definitely.

"So, you see. I do know. Ready?"

"You go first. I'm still trying to catch my breath."

He chuckled and fumbled in the dark for the doorknob. When there was light he checked to see how well he'd dressed in the dark, opened the door a little farther to check the traffic in the hall, then stepped out.

"Why, Ms. Miller," he said, turning in the open door, his voice echoing as he extended a hand to her. He was grinning when she took it, his other hand reaching out to straighten a few stray curls. He looped her hand over the bend in his arm, gave the closet door a shove with his foot, before he led her down the hallway, saying, "*Really* glad you could make it this afternoon."

"Wouldn't have missed it for the *world*, Mr. Hammond."

EIGHT

"I don't know, baby girl," he said, watching his daughter turn red in the face from screaming. "It's hot today. She's got her windows closed, and I bet the air conditioner's on. She probably wouldn't hear us anyway."

"When she stops playing, she'll hear us," Chloe insisted. "Do you think she'll play the one where the little girl paints her room red again?"

"Probably. If you ask her with a please, I think she might."

"It's pretty, isn't it, Daddy?" she said of the muffled music coming from the house next door. She rested her arms across the clean, white, freshly painted windowsill to cushion her chin, closing her eyes to make pictures in her head.

He stroked her thick, straight black hair, his hand covering most of her head like a baseball cap. For the millionth time since she was born, he marveled at the miracle of her and pondered the mystery of how she came to be his.

"Yes. It's very pretty," he said, his gaze falling to Gus's dining room window. Her back was to them, her violin under her chin so that her face was angled toward them as she stood before a music stand practicing. "Very, very pretty."

Another miracle to contemplate. He didn't know what it was, but he must have done something very right in his life to have been given this second chance at happiness. He sighed and rested his elbow on the sill to support his chin as he watched her. How did so much talent and beauty and sweetness get stuffed into one small package like that, he puzzled. So much woman. So much heart.

It wasn't just her music she put her all into, it was everything she thought was worth doing. Teaching the children. Her house. The meals she cooked. Her conversations with Chloe. Her love for him. She was no halfway woman. No failure.

What she thought of as her failures served only to make her stronger as a person, shaping her character with a unique perspective of other people, sharpening her empathy for them, honing her compassion.

He saw it all the time when she was with Chloe. Saw it when she spoke of other people, always intimating that they were doing the best they could with what they had. She was a private, introverted person, but it was no surprise to know that those who knew her thought highly of her, loved her dearly.

"Okay, Daddy, she's stopping again. Ready?"

"You bet. But wouldn't it be a lot easier to call her on the phone?"

"Next door?" she asked, incredulous. "When we can see her right there?"

Okay. He was a moron.

"You say the one-two-three," she said. He did, and then they both bellowed, "Aaaaaa-gus-taaaaa." Twice.

Nothing.

"Oh! Oh," he said. "Wait right here. I have an idea."

"Augusta Miller." Her name boomed through the silence from nowhere, as if God Himself were speaking to her. "We know you're in there. Open your window and keep your hands where we can see them."

Her face agog, Gus finally turned to the window, looked low and then high, and found Chloe and Scotty laughing at her from a second-story window.

"We know you can hear us. Put down your violin. Slowly. You cooperate with us and no one'll get hurt," he said, speaking into a red-and-white megaphone. What the neighbors were thinking . . . she didn't really care. All she could see was Chloe's face and she was having too much fun.

"Give yourself up and we'll go easy on ya," he added.

Laughing, she went to the dining room window and opened it wide.

"I surrender," she called up to them. "Does that make me as crazy as the two of you?"

"Let me do it, Daddy." He passed the horn to Chloe. Holding Gus's gaze, he mouthed "I love you." "Gus. This is Chloe. Can you hear me now? I want to come over to your house. Okay?"

Behind her, Scotty was holding up ten fingers, flashing them twice to indicate he'd follow her over in twenty minutes.

"Sure, it's okay," she hollered back. "I've been hoping you'd come to visit. I'll meet you at the gate."

"Okay. Good-bye," she said, handing the horn back to her father and disappearing from the window, not even noticing the smiles and special looks being exchanged by the two adults.

"Hi," Chloe said a few short minutes later as she and Bert walked through the gate into Gus's backyard. "You sure did look funny when we were calling to you."

"Well, I thought the police were after me. I thought I was in big trouble." This delighted Chloe. "And then there you were, and I'd just been thinking about you."

"You were?"

"Yes. I was hoping I'd get to see you before you went back to Springfield. I wanted to thank you for inviting me to go to the park with you and your daddy yesterday. I had a really good time."

"Me, too, except there was no music like Daddy said."

"Well, he just got the date wrong," Gus said, knowing the girl had been dispirited, but not realizing how much. "I didn't know you liked bluegrass music, Chloe. I'll have to get some tapes and—"

"I don't," she said. "I don't even know it. I just wanted to dance on the blue grass, and surprise my daddy."

Gus frowned. "The grass isn't really blue, honey. Bluegrass is a kind of music. Like rock 'n' roll or Western music. It's just a different kind of music."

"Oh." This was discouraging, but not the whole problem. "Then I guess I could have danced anywhere."

"Well, sure. I'd love to see you dance, but how were you going to surprise your daddy?"

Chloe looked back toward her house and then stepped closer to Gus to whisper, "I'm taking lessons."

Gus let her eyes grow round. "Dancing lessons? And your daddy doesn't know yet?"

"I wanted to surprise him. Mommy said it would be a good one."

"She's right. It will be." She hesitated. "But you don't really need music, do you? You can still surprise him."

Chloe scrunched up her face and started to shake her head.

"It's not the same. My teacher has records and sometimes she plays the piano when I dance, and it's better."

"Oh. Well, do you know the name of the song? Does it have to be piano music?"

"Sure I know it. I can sing it too. I dance and I sing and everything."

"Oh, well, we don't want your daddy to miss that. Maybe you could sing it for me, I might know it."

Chloe put one small arm in the air and the other on her hip, wiggled a little, shuffled her feet till she had them where she wanted them, then began, "I'm a little teapot—"

"Oh, Chloe," she broke in. "I do know that one. Stay right here."

Returning moments later with her violin, she found Chloe and Bert laying on their stomachs in the grass waiting for her, one of them was picking petals off a daisy.

"Would you like to take some of those home to your mommy?" she asked, recalling the first time she saw Chloe. She was like a daisy—sweet, innocent, unaffected.

"Okay."

There were several clumps of daisies that still had fresh blooms, though it was late in the season. Chloe looked them over carefully, snapping the heads off a couple before Gus showed her how to get the longer stems. They had a neat little pile of them by the time Scotty showed up.

"You two aren't hard to find," he said, coming through the gate. "I just follow the giggles and there you are." He tackled Chloe, taking her down softly. "What's so funny, huh?"

She laughed and rolled with the tender punches. "Gus," she gasped, laughing. "Gus has two left feet."

"She does?" he stopped to look at her with no little interest. "Let's see 'em."

With her knees bent, she placed her feet flat on the grass in front of her, the skirt of her dress hiding everything from the ankles up.

He frowned at them, took each one in hand and brought them to his lap. He turned them back and forth, caressed them, sent shivers up her spine when he ran his hands up and down her legs. "I don't know, Chlo. They look right to me."

"That's what I said," she said. "But inside they're both left and they act dumb. Gus can't dance cuz her two left feet dance the wrong way."

"Awww," he said sadly. "That's too bad." His eyes were warm and intimate when they met hers. "Maybe she just needs to practice. We'll work on that next time. You and I'll teach poor ol' Gus to dance," he said, holding her gaze as he pressed his thumbs into her instep, kneading and . . . needing.

"We can start now," Chloe said, jumping up. "I can teach her. I can dance. Wanna see me?"

He smiled at her enthusiasm, then glanced at his watch. "No time, baby girl. We have to get going."

"Oh no," Gus said quickly, shooting him a look. "There's time. Plenty of time. I want to see Chloe dance. Oh! And I just happen to have my violin here. How about some music to dance to, Chloe."

The little girl grinned, put one small arm in the air and the other on her hip, wiggled a little, shuffled her feet till she had them where she wanted them. Gus positioned her instrument, and with a teacher's practiced body language gave a short introduction and the nod to go.

Brush-brush stepping and belting out the words to the nursery song, Chloe went through the hand motions and pirouettes, tipping sideways at the end—the whole routine lasting less than two minutes.

"Good night!" Scotty said, appropriately astonished and awed by her great talent. "Where did you learn to do that?"

Enthralled with herself, Chloe bounced across the lawn into his lap and, with wild hand movements and sparkling dark eyes, told him all about her lessons.

Gus, with her violin in her lap, sighed and leaned back on her arms to watch them. She couldn't stop the sharp stab of envy that pierced her. It wasn't merely the father-daughter portrait she was watching . . . and missing. It went beyond that. Where did such absolute faith and unquestioning love come from? Would he always be her hero? Would she always be one fabulous surprise after another for him? The answer was so obviously yes, she had to blink back tears.

If she had a daughter or a son? This wasn't the first time she'd felt the yearning inside her, but she couldn't remember it ever being so strong or feeling it so desperately. How could anything—anyone—as loving and giving, joyous and pure, as bright and earnest as a child *ever* be a disappointment? Not a perfect child. A human child, always testing and learning, making mistakes and growing . . . always needing love and understanding and giving it in kind. Where

was the disappointment in that? Mistakes and failures—they were expected, weren't they? To learn, to
develop character, to keep life from getting too . . .
blah? Monotonous and flat? Taken for granted?

She smiled and closed her eyes when Chloe
hugged her and kissed her good-bye. She grinned
when Scotty winked his farewell and made a promise
of a speedy return, and watched them walk away hand
in hand, the mirror of each other's life. The hopes.
The dreams. The attitudes. Even some of the man-
nerisms.

She wondered at the reflections she and her
mother made of each other. If her mother looked at
something with disappointment, did she see it as well?

He hadn't missed the mushy I-want-a-baby glow
in Gus's eyes earlier. It haunted him all the way
home. She haunted him.

There were times when bills piled up and times
when he brushed elbows with men who owned cars
they rarely drove, who had their children's futures se-
cured in trust funds, who'd seen Madagascar and
cruised the Indian Ocean. There were times when he
knew he could have been one of those men, even an
occasion or two when he wished he was.

But he was meant to be a simple man. He found
his greatest joy in touching the lives of young people,
his greatest hopes in the people he loved, his excitement in the procreation of life, and his contentment
in protecting it.

The idea of filling Gus's belly with life excited him. He dreamed of doing it a couple of times and then spending the rest of his life re-creating those moments of delirious happiness with her as they watched their children grow.

He wanted what his parents had. Was that so bad? He didn't think so. Their life together had been busy and productive, filled with laughter and love. What else was there? Ambition to have more than you needed? Power to generate respect or influence from other people? Altruism to make a difference in the world, to write history, to change the day?

He smiled as he pulled into the driveway between his house and hers. Well, who was to say he didn't have it all already? That he wasn't influencing people, making a difference, changing the day? Life didn't have to be complicated to be good.

If Gus didn't know what he knew, if she wasn't conscious of it, she at least felt the same way. He saw it in the satisfaction she took in her garden, when she played her music, when she was with her students, when she sat quietly and listened to night noises, when she raced out after an autumn shower to smell the air and went barefoot in the grass at the park.

He got out of the car and headed for the front porch light she'd left on for him, smiling. Moments later he sighed, relieved and easy, as he held her in his arms, slow dancing to some weird classical tune she'd been listening to when he came in.

The sound of her laughter washed over him like

grace from God when he twirled her round and round, her body tight and warm against his.

"What's gotten into you?" she asked, breathing quick, her pretty green eyes casting rays of the love and happiness she was feeling upon his soul.

"I'm crazy about you," he said, dipping her back over his arm. "Left feet and all. Marry me."

"What?"

"Marry me, Gus. You and I, we're what happily ever after is all about. We have it all." He tipped her upright, met her mouth with his. "Marry me. Share the rest of your life with me. Grow old with me. Let me love you. Let me . . ." He frowned, then glanced down at the hands pushing him away.

He didn't let go of her, but he stopped talking long enough for her to ask, "You're serious?"

"As a snakebite. As a heart attack. As taxes."

"Scotty . . ."

"As a review board. As a born-again minister in the middle of the week. As a . . ."

"Scotty!"

He laughed. "I'm serious. Gus, we're perfect for each other. We want the same things. You've made me happier than I ever dreamed I could be. I love you."

"Oh, Scotty," she said, finally slipping from his hold and moving away, her heart aching more with each step. "We barely know each other." He still thought she was someone special. "It's only been a few weeks." She hadn't had time to screw anything up yet, to disappoint him. "This is a big step." And he'd hate her if she let him make it before he had time to get a clearer, truer picture of her.

He laughed at the confusion and mild panic in her expression.

"It's a huge step," he said, throwing his arms wide, then lunging and closing them around her. "And I'm not being fair, am I? I knew, almost the first time I laid eyes on you, I knew we'd end up together eventually. I was never this sure the first time, with Jan. It wasn't like this. I loved her, but . . . I never saw us growing old together, never saw us with children." Then, as if it just occurred to him, he added, "Maybe that's why Chloe was such a surprise—a wonderful, unexpected surprise."

"You were busy dreaming about other things when she was born. You were younger, had your whole life . . ."

"No," he said, turning her as he sat down on the couch, pulling her down onto his lap. "I've always seen myself with children, and growing old with someone I love. Even as a kid." Slowly and with much consideration, he started to unbutton the front of her dress. He liked this dress, an off-white with tiny yellow flowers and green leaves the same color as her eyes. "But we don't have to talk about this now, if it's making you uncomfortable. I guess I . . ." He looked up into her face. "I wanted you to know how I was feeling, I guess. Hoping you'd tell me what was on your mind too." She grimaced and tipped her head to one side. "But you don't have to . . ."

She used the back of the couch to turn herself and

straddle his lap, taking his face in her hands and kissing him tenderly once, then once again.

"Not that I'm ever planning to get old, mind you—but if I were, you're the only man I'd want to grow old with. And if I ever have children, I hope they'll be yours," she said, kissing him again as his fingers continued to work her buttons. "I'm just having a really hard time believing how happy I am right now. I didn't see this coming. I didn't know it could be like this. Do we have to rush? Can't we go slow and enjoy it?"

He smiled. Knowing she was happy was enough, for now. He parted the gap he'd made in her dress, rose up, and meticulously placed kisses along the line of her bra to the valley between her breasts, breathing in the scent of mystery and passion hidden there. Desire plowed through him, hard and fast. Go slow and enjoy, he told himself, drawing a line up her breastbone with his tongue, nipping at her throat.

Relief seeped into her with the first wave of excited anticipation that jellied her bones and sent her pulse racing. There was time yet—to love him, to touch him, to wallow in his affections before it all came crashing down around her again. Time was all she was asking for, and a little good luck. She would horde the memories of moments like this, cherish them for the long nights when she felt like what they'd shared was nothing more than one of those dreams he'd spoken of.

"No," he said finally. "We don't have to rush anything." Taking her by the shoulders, he lowered her to the couch, resuming his work on her buttons. "In fact—"

"Scotty."

"Shhhhh . . ." He pulled one hand slowly down her chest to her belly, while the other continued to slip buttons from their holes. "Don't talk. Let me make love to you. I want to watch your eyes get dark and—"

"Scotty . . ."

He leaned over and placed a hot kiss in her navel, laved it with his tongue. ". . . feel you tremble in my arms and—"

"Scotty?"

"Mmm?"

"This one has a zipper. In back."

He looked at the buttons he was fiddling with above her pelvis, felt her stomach quiver with laughter, then lifted his face to hers. She bit down hard on her lower lip to keep from laughing, but it was too late.

". . . and tickle you till you scream for mercy!"

Laughing and screaming, panting and tumbling, they wrestled on the couch, then rolled onto the floor kicking and squirming. He topped her, capturing both her hands in one of his above her head.

"You try my patience, Ms. Miller." She giggled. "Buttons and zippers and hooks. What I should do, is chain you naked to a bed. Have my way with you whenever I want, no fuss, no muss."

"How dull," she said, the amusement in her eyes turning seductive and insightful. Intrigued, he loosened his grip on her hands. They came forward immediately. "I love undressing you." She started with his belt buckle. "You're so warm." Her hands under his shirt were the evidence. "I love the way your stomach quivers when I touch it. I like counting your ribs and feeling your heart beating here, under my palm. The muscles and your shoulders, so wide, make me feel safe and weak at the same time." She sat up, and he leaned back on his feet as she continued pushing the shirt and his arms upward. "And these muscles in your arms . . . mmm . . . I love it when you hold me."

He flipped his shirt off his wrists, tossing it blindly. His gaze was snagged on hers when he peeled her dress away from her.

"Who's seducing who here?" he asked absently, his eyes lowering to drink in the sight of her breasts as he uncovered them.

"Hard to tell, isn't it?" she answered, smiling, meeting his glance with shining love and a desire as hot as the hinges of hell.

The line between seducer and seducee was tissue thin, and who was whom, was never firmly established as they made slow sweet love to each other. Legs hairy and smooth tangled, muscles large and small strained and relaxed in turn. Hands big and dainty soothed and teased indiscriminately. Teeth nipped at the soft skin and wet lips taunted coarse, unpolished instincts as old and as primitive and as unfailing as a sunrise.

He propelled her to the edge of oblivion, gave her

time to consider the jump, then pushed her off and watched her fall before taking the leap himself. He was there to catch her when she landed, his arms cradling her weak, sweetly tortured body. Warm and secure.

"Why didn't we do this in bed?" he wondered aloud, exhausted and too listless to move.

"I told you we'd be sorry if we didn't," she muttered.

He frowned and opened his eyes, trying to recall her saying those words.

"As I remember it, you said you loved undressing me, and I couldn't keep your hands off me. You attacked me, and we didn't have time to get to a bed."

"Humph. What was I supposed to do? You were diddling with all those buttons when there was a perfectly good zipper."

His chest rocked with silent laughter. "I think you should look into muumuus, something that just slips over your head like a T-shirt."

"I think you should slow down and start checking for zippers."

"I think we're gonna die here."

"I think we might."

"I think . . . I could live with that," he said, smiling when she laughed softly.

"I think," she said, sticking with the game but changing the subject, "Chloe would make an adorable Munchkin."

The hand he was brushing up and down her arm stopped.

"Ya think?"

"Don't you?"

He went silent a moment to let the idea swim through the bog that was once his brain. "I'd be including her in my life. *She'd* love it. You'd teach her the songs?" He tipped his head a bit and looked at her with one eye open.

"Of course. And I was thinking earlier that she might feel awkward—being an outsider, but I counted four of her cousins on my Munchkin list, and I was thinking I'd work with the Mayor and the boys in the Lollipop Guild separately. She could meet them too."

"I *think* you did a lot of thinking about this," he said, his tone light, his heart heavy with emotion.

A slight shrug. "She was just so cute out there this afternoon, dancing and singing for you. Showing off for you. This would be another opportunity for her."

"And little girls should have plenty of opportunities to show off for their daddies, right?"

She nodded. He took her chin in two fingers, tipping her head, forcing her to look back at him. Dark eyes, abysmal in their ability to perceive, he searched her face softly, tenderly. He traced her lower lip with his thumb, her cheek with the back of one finger. He stroked her hair from her face, delving deeply into the cool green pools of her eyes. For a moment she thought he was going to say something, then he simply pulled her close and held her tight, as if he'd plucked her from the edge of a cliff, terrified of losing her.

NINE

It was argued early on that perhaps a winter or spring production might give them more time to prepare, but Scotty had insisted that the cold and flu season after Christmas would have kids dropping out like flies and that spring was too busy with college fever and other senior rites to get their full attention.

Therefore, Tylerville's First Annual Senior Play was scheduled to open for a two-night run the weekend before Thanksgiving. They had eight weeks.

Eight weeks was *more* than enough time, he said. But of course, only a Midas Man would think this way.

Relatively speaking, Gus had very little to do, but she went about it in her usual style—methodically, from the beginning. First, she brought popcorn and ginger ale to school and watched the entire movie with the children: ground zero; everyone starting out on the right foot; basic understanding of the project.

The next day she played only the Munchkin scene for them—step two, focus on a specific area. On the third day she held auditions for speaking and singing parts, which was step three, dividing the specific area of focus into controllable subsections. Day four, she delegated responsibility, handing out sheets of paper with the words to the songs on them and doing a quick run through of the three songs they'd be doing: "Come Out, Come Out, Wherever You Are." "Ding! Dong! The Witch Is Dead." And "Welcome to Munchkin Land."

For the next six weeks they rehearsed the songs. All the Munchkins stayed after school for an hour on Tuesdays and Thursdays. The Lullaby League, Lollipop Guild, the Mayor, the Bishop, and the Coroner staying Wednesdays as well.

Scotty, on the other hand, had his own methodology—putting all his sticks in the pot at once.

Rather than use a production company's version of *The Wizard of Oz*, which included the little heard of Jitterbugs in the Enchanted Forest and called for a magic bridge that no one born after 1939 could identify with—and for maximum educational benefit—Scotty decided to stick as close to the Judy Garland movie version of the story as possible.

And so . . . Auditions for the lead singing roles were being held by the band director, even as Mrs. Fiske and her volunteers in the English department wrote the first draft of the script while Carolann Goreman, the over-sexed biology teacher, and her five-student committee of choreographers watched over their shoulders for ideas. Scotty finagled lumber from the local hardware store owner and turned it over to the physical education department. The football coach and his horde, which included several browbeaten parents as well as students, were in charge of building the sets according to the designs provided by Jayne Nivens and her troupe of artists—who also painted them when they were finished. With the basketball coach and his posse of prop procurers turning the town upside down, Scotty was dazzling Diane Watts out of all the remnants in her fabric store and taunting Lester Finch, who was not to be outdone, into donating a whole bolt of green brocade drapery material for the good citizens of Emerald City.

"There are fifty Munchkins total," he announced to the ladies and gentlemen at Shady Grove Retirement Home. "They're all pretty much the same size, so we thought a one-size-fits-most pattern would work out well. You could cut them out three or four at a time and set up something like an assembly line, if you think that would be easier for you. The few that will need bigger or small costumes, or special costumes like the Lollipop Guild, are being taken care of by Carrie Mutrux, the minister's wife, who's working closely with Augusta Miller, who's in charge of all the Munchkins," he said, swinging his arms wide. "Yes, Mr. Hayes, you have a question?"

"I just want to check this out, for sure. You say you'll send a bus for us, for the closing-night performance? And we get a ten-percent senior citizens discount on the tickets? And all we have to do is make fifty costumes?"

"That's what I said," he answered like a circus hawker. "Plus an exclusive performance right here at the home, by the Munchkins . . . a sort of pre–dress-rehearsal rehearsal for them."

The old man puckered his mouth and nodded twice before he said, "Count me in. Pass me a needle and thread."

"You old fool," the woman sitting beside him muttered. "You can't see anything smaller than a barn. How you gonna see the eye of a needle?"

"Huh. If that's true, then it's no wonder I can see you plain as day."

"That's enough," a woman named Sally Garvey announced with a clear tone of authority Scotty was glad to hear. There was one in every crowd, he'd discovered over the years, a take-over-and-organize-things person, who . . . took over and organized things. "George, you can see well enough to press the costumes once they're finished. Now, who else is in on this?"

Scotty smiled and sighed over another job well done as Sally called for nonarthritic volunteers to cut out the patterns and assigned elastic threading to another farsighted resident. He was off to Phillips Lighting and Electric to see what could be wrangled for the lighting board at the high school, which was in dire need of some repairs.

"Okay, we have the ladies of the Garden Club doing the Kansas costumes. The Ladies Auxiliary is taking care of the Oz costumes for the lead characters, and the Daughters of the Pioneers are handling the Emerald City getups," he said, rattling off missions accomplished as he checked them off the list on his clipboard one evening in Gus's living room. He had removed his shoes and propped his feet up on her coffee table—papers, magazines, and books scattered about him in a three-foot radius. "Jerry Divine, our illustrious guidance counselor, is working with his kids, designing the tickets, flyers, and programs. And the guy at Paper and Prints said he'd give us a really good deal on the printing. So, that leaves . . . hmmm . . . that's it," he muttered, frowning over his list. "All we have left is to figure out what to do about the cast party and . . . What?" he asked, glancing up to find Gus scowling at him.

"Midas Man, my aunt Fanny," she said, with much mock disgust. "You're nothing but a wheeler-dealer, an operator, a flimflammer, a plain old hustler."

"And your point is?"

"You," she said, nodding her head. "You."

He raised one brow, tossed his clipboard aside, and waited, giving her another chance to make her statement.

"You've got nearly everyone in this town working on this play that was *your* idea."

"Yes?"

"Conning construction materials, pitting merchants against one another for bigger and bigger contributions, inducting slave labor with a promise here and a ticket discount there."

"All without a single drop of blood drawn, I might add."

"You're like the Music Man and the Rain Maker and . . . and . . ."

"And?"

"And . . . I'm very impressed," she said, releasing her smile. "It's not a senior play anymore, it's a community project. Single-handedly, you've pulled everyone in this town into this, into a tight-knit unit with a single cause. It's . . ."

Could it be? It was something she never thought she'd see. Scotty looked away, fingered the papers on the couch beside him while his neck and face grew rosy and hot.

"You're blushing!"

"I am not."

"You are," she said, getting out of her chair, remaining bent over as she approached him for a better look. "You are. Praise embarrasses you." She was close enough now to touch his face with one finger. She snapped it back and blew on it, as if it were burned. "Oh! This is so cute. The Great White Scotty Hammond all hot and pink, blushing like a— ahhhhh!"

Quick as a hiccup, he reached out and snatched her, pulling her down atop his papers and books.

"You're not laughing at me, are you?" he asked menacingly, pinning her arms at her sides.

"Me? No. Never." She laughed.

"Good. Because you know what happens to people who laugh at me."

"Oh no. Not the Chinese tickle torture."

With a hazardous light in his eyes, he nodded. "Exactly. Now, was I blushing?"

"Well . . ." She felt the pressure of his thumbs at her ribs. "I thought maybe for a second you might be, but obviously I was wrong."

Again he nodded, looking satisfied, a smirk on his lips. "It takes a big person to admit when they're wrong," he said, repositioning himself a little so he could reward her with a kiss. "I love a woman who can admit she's wrong."

"You do?"

"I do," he said, moving in slowly, feeling her anticipation and prolonging it, until his own was unbearable. He brushed his lips against hers, teasing and testing until he felt her teeth nipping at his lower lip. He deepened the kiss, sliding a hand beneath her and pushing everything under her onto the floor.

She looped her freed arms around his neck and let him carry her away to a place she'd come to know as "our place," where only the two of them existed and reality gave way to magic. Her breath caught in her throat when his mouth closed over the rapid-fire pulse at the base of her neck, and she murmured, "And I love a man who can blush."

Truth was, she was relieved to know she was in love with just a man. A simple man. Let the gossips say what they wanted. Let the town fathers believe what they liked. She knew Scotty Hammond's secret.

And his secret was as simple as he was. It was hard work. He didn't leap tall buildings in a single bound, he took the stairs like everyone else—he just never let anyone see him sweat.

By Halloween, Gus was ready to try a couple rehearsals in the high school auditorium on Saturday mornings.

"That's okay, Jeremy. You make as many rehearsals as you can, when they don't interfere with your soccer games," she told the nineteenth child who had come to her with this same concern. She stood up and waved her arms at the Munchkins onstage. "Boys and girls? May I have your attention please? These Saturday morning rehearsals are to get you used to being on the stage . . ." and to a lesser extent to give Chloe a chance to sing and become friendly with the group, ". . . and to make sure you're singing loud enough for the people in the last row to hear you. That's very important. I understand that many of you have soccer games and that basketball is starting up and some of you older children have midget football on Saturdays, so just make as many of these rehearsals as you can. Okay? We'll still practice the songs at school, and later on I'll be giving you a schedule of the days when we'll be rehearsing with the high school people. So until then, just come when you can and try not to worry too much."

She watched Carrie Mutrux herd several strays out of the wings and back onstage, and smiled to herself.

She really loved working with these children. They were so young and so easily distracted, and yet they poured all their enthusiasm into singing the songs, were very serious about being the best Munchkins they could be, and worried constantly about doing everything *right*. There wasn't a conductor anywhere who wouldn't have given his or her eyeteeth for a group so willing and eager to please.

"Okay, we have a few more minutes before your parents come to pick you up, so let's try the 'Follow the Yellow Brick Road' song. Remember, Dorothy will be walking in a bigger and bigger circle, so you need to stay out of her way. Mrs. Mutrux will be Dorothy today, and where are my three speakers?"

Two hands rose in the back, and Chloe jumped out of the crowd saying, "I'm right here, Gus."

"Good. Now all three of you listen for your cues and say, 'follow the yellow brick road,' real loud. Okay?" She pressed the play button on the tape recorder when they were all in place. "Get ready now . . ." she said, then lowered her hand on the down beat.

The song was all of two lines long, repeated once with a lead into "We're Off to See the Wizard." Gus clapped wildly at the end. "You are the best Munchkins ever," she announced.

She gathered up the temporary props and her belongings as parents came for their children, asked about soccer games and where to purchase tickets, and eventually left Carrie, Gus, and Chloe in the auditorium alone.

"Thanks for all your help, Carrie. I could never handle all this alone."

"Are you kidding. I'm having a ball. Every time the Lollipop Guild sings, every time I *think* of them singing, I laugh. They are so darling. And I'm so proud of myself. I've been looking for striped tights for their costumes, and I finally found some the other day in Springfield when I went over to visit my mother."

"I live in Springfield," Chloe said, assuming her share of the conversation as the three of them walked toward the exit. "With my mommy."

"I know you do, darlin'. And I think it was such a good idea of your daddy's to let you be in the play. Now you'll have friends in Springfield and friends in Tylerville too."

"I know," she said. "But Daddy said it was Gus's idea for me to be a Munchkin, and Mommy said it was a good thing Daddy had Gus."

"Did she?" Carrie asked, encouraging the child to tell more, even as she sent Gus a wily glance. "Because Gus has so many good ideas?"

Chloe looked at an apprehensive Gus. "I guess so, but mostly we're glad because we don't want Daddy to be lonely all by himself."

"I see," Carrie said, grinning at Gus, who sighed audibly. "So your daddy and Gus are spending lots of time together, are they?"

"I guess so. Daddy says being with Gus makes him happy." She hesitated. "But being with Gus *and* me makes him happiest of all."

"Your daddy's a lucky man to have you, Chloe," Carrie said sincerely before turning to Gus, knowing and amused.

"I know." Chloe slipped her hand into Gus's. "And so is Gus."

That was debatable for the next week or so when rooms would go suddenly silent with Gus's arrival and any mention of Scott Hammond would get her a nudge and a congratulatory grin. Though she confirmed and denied nothing, they were soon paired up like peanut butter and jelly, a cough and a cold, warm milk and insomnia . . . like Bertrum T. Goodfellow and barbecue-flavored Dog-Gone Dog Yummies.

"How long did you think we could conceal it in a town this size?" he asked, studying what was left of the warm milk she'd made for herself and poured into a glass for him.

Now, Bert didn't mind a little nighttime roaming. As a matter of fact, he'd just finished his midnight security check when the woman stumbled out of the bedroom. The little one did it frequently to take in and let out fluids, so he was used to it. But the man was up now too. The light over the stove was on. Beverages were prepared. And they were talking. Really, it was too inconsiderate, he decided with a huffy snort. He curled up under the table to wait them out. He was not a happy puppy.

"People were bound to find out eventually."

"I know," she said, sitting across her kitchen table from him, her left hand in her lap, going around and around. Now when she failed him, the whole town would know that as well. She'd had a nightmare about the looks and the turning heads, the cold shoulders and pitying pats on the arm she'd endured the last time she'd failed. Warm milk was a poor substitute for the regime of antidepressant drug therapy she was beginning to feel she might need. "I just thought there would be more time."

The milk in his glass had grown a skin and taken on a life of its own, so he set it aside.

"Time for what?" he asked, his expression gentle with understanding. "Just the two of us? To cocoon ourselves in our little secret? In our own little world?" He slipped the tips of his fingers under hers. "I admit, I'm going to miss those looks across a crowded room, our surreptitious meetings, but it'll be nice to hold your hand in public too. Take you to the movies. Go to dinner in romantic restaurants . . ."

But couldn't he see how much worse that would make everything when she let him down? When he couldn't bear the sight of her any longer and yet he'd let everyone know how he'd once felt by taking her out in public? She couldn't tolerate the thought of his humiliation.

"What about your reputation?"

"My what?" He laughed.

"You're the principal of the high school. People look up to you, they trust you to set a good example for—"

Again he laughed. "What? You think I'll strip you down in the park so we can make love in the fountain?" He hesitated. "I don't think anyone would put that past me, come to think of it, but the fact is, they knew I was a red-blooded single male when they hired me. Now, I don't intend to do anything so scandalous as to attack you on the school playground, but I also have no intention of living the life of a monk, just because I'm the principal. I'm a man. A human being. I'm in love, and I'm proud of it."

She sighed loudly and melted all over the Formica tabletop. He didn't play fair. She saw the unsuspecting sincerity in his expression, then shook her head and lowered her eyes away from it. He wouldn't understand until it happened. They were a slow-motion train wreck in the making: two locomotives on close parallel tracks, heading in the same direction, equal in size and strength, seemingly safe—with track missing up ahead.

"Come on, Gus," he said after several minutes of watching her stew. "It won't be so bad. And it's certainly nothing to lose sleep over. Come back to bed, and I'll help you forget all about it." She smiled when she looked up and found him staring lecherously, wagging his brows. "Truly. This is what small towns are all about. The babies grow up, fall in love, get married, have babies of their own. In another week, the two of us will be old news."

Wanting very much to believe him, and ignoring the potential of any and all events bringing them suddenly back as front-page news, she began to climb out of her muddy pit of despair—only to recall the approach of another impending disaster which had her slipping back to the bottom.

"In another week my mother will be here."

He couldn't help laughing at the dread in her voice and on her face. "Want me to warm up more milk?"

"You wait. You meet my mother and then try to laugh."

"Listen, the whole time she's here I'll be wearing my shining armor. All you have to do is squeak in distress, and I'll come running to rescue you."

She simpered and nodded at him. "And who's going to rescue you?"

He looked appalled. "Me? Ha! She's gonna *luuuv* me."

"Hmmm. Think you're pretty slick, don't ya?"

"As frog fur." He flashed his dimples at her to prove his point. He pried her empty milk glass from her hands, drew her to her feet, and placed her hand in the bend of his arm. "I don't know how you missed noticing it, but I happen to be a *huge* hit with the over-forty crowd." He was also a huge hit with the under-forty crowd, but why split hairs, she thought. "I'm as irresistible as a rumba on Saturday night," he said, twirling her into the bedroom. His boxers could just as easily have been a tux with tails as he caught her and took her down for *the dip.* "As overpowering as apple pie à la mode," he added, dropping kisses along her throat. "As beguiling as all things warm and fuzzy."

"Actually," she said, laughing as she fell onto the bed with him. "I did notice."

◆━━━━━━━━◆

"You are the best sister I've ever had."

"Remember that the next time Alan and I want to go to the beach for a month, alone," Lydia said, verbalizing her favorite haggard-young-mother fantasy. "Which could very well be the day after Thanksgiving when Mother leaves. I told Eric he'd be sleeping in Jake and Todd's room for a little while, and he broke out in a rash. I didn't even have to tell him why."

"Aw, poor guy. I know exactly how he feels. But if he's that upset . . ."

"I'm kidding. Besides, it makes more sense for her to stay here with us. You're gone all day. God knows what she'd find to get involved in without constant supervision."

"That's true. Lord, what if she volunteers to help with the play?"

"It's too late. Everyone in town has a job to do for it, there aren't any left. She'll just have to sit passively in the audience."

"Well, at least that will be something to look forward to. Mother passive. Mother with nothing to do. I— Hang on, Liddy, someone's at the door."

Not time for a violin lesson. Not Scotty or Chloe, because they always used the back door. She was curious, and glancing out the front window, she saw no car out front.

"Mother!"

"Augusta, honey, help me with this, will you?"

Wanda Miller said, breathlessly hoisting a heavy cardboard box at her daughter. "Can you believe the cab driver wouldn't tote it into the house for me? He just set everything there on the sidewalk." She dropped a quick kiss on Gus's cheek before she reached out the door to drag in a large suitcase. "The world is going to hell in a handbasket, I'm telling you. No one has any manners anymore. Men think the gentle part of gentleman is a synonym for gay, and most of them won't have anything to do with it." She stopped short and looked at her. "What have you been up to, sweetie? You look lovely."

"I do? I mean, what . . ."

"Now, I know we all agreed that I'd stay at Lydia's, but I was thinking about it, and with the play and Thanksgiving coming up, she doesn't need me underfoot, and I think I should divide myself evenly when I come to visit anyway. I know you're quiet and set in your ways, but I promise I won't interfere. Oh, I love the color you chose for this room. What is it? Peach?"

"Dainty Apricot."

"Apples and oranges," she said, laughing as she hauled her suitcase to the middle of the room, dropping it like a ton of bricks. "I was close."

Gus shuffled the heavy box to a chair and set it down. "What's in this?"

"Fifty-six hundred copies of *It's My Rain Forest Too*. One for everyone in town," she said, still marveling at the paint. "And you did all this work yourself?"

"Yes." She looked around the room as if she'd

never seen it before. She felt vague and confused. "Most of it."

"You still need drapes, I see, but I imagine you're taking your time and picking out the exact right colors. I'm so parched. Honey, can I bother you for some tea? I hate to admit it, but my nerves aren't what they used to be. I remember a time when I thought a bus ride from Seattle to Muskogee, Oklahoma, and then on to Augusta, Georgia, and back again in the heat of the summer to attend a couple Civil Rights rallies was a lark—and now an eighty-minute plane ride just frazzles me."

"Well . . . yes. Of course. Tea? Ah, right. I didn't even ask how your trip was, Mother," she said, as if she'd had a chance to. "Oh dear, I left Liddy on the phone. Come . . . come into the kitchen. That way. You can say hello to her while I heat the water."

Listening to her mother reexplain her independent thinking to Lydia was like watching reruns of the first O.J. Simpson trial, but ten times more frustrating.

It was one unbelievable little complication after another. Two weeks without sex notwithstanding, she wasn't looking forward to being interrogated about Scotty or the long evenings of empty conversation as they both skirted all subjects that might brush on the failure of her musical career or the tense moments of heavy innuendo pertaining to her contributions to society . . . albeit Tylerville's.

This as she actively waited for the blight of her life to have its inevitable effect on what was fast becoming the one thing in her life she didn't think she could bear to fail at—her future with Scotty Hammond. How much more could she deal with?

"Gus! Gus!" Chloe shouted, blasting through the back door without her usual ring on the bell. "Guess what I got? Just guess. I get to keep her here at Daddy's house. Guess what it is. Guess *where* it is." She laughed excitedly. "Just guess." Spotting Wanda two feet away on the phone, she frowned a moment, then asked, "Who's that on your phone?"

"That's my mother, Chloe. Mother," she said, noting the keen interest she was taking in the child. "This is Chloe Hammond from next door."

"How do you do, Chloe?" she said, smiling.

"I'm doing real good. Guess what I got? Guess where it is?"

"All right. One moment, Lydia. Chloe?" she said, bending low, playing the game like a pro. "What have you got? And where is it?"

Chloe laughed again, putting both hands in the muff-pocket of her hooded sweatshirt. "You'll never guess," she chortled. "I got a mouse in my pocket. See."

Though the mouse was hardly much bigger than Chloe's fist, the thin pink tail dangling long and rat-like from the bottom, it was the unexpectedness of it that triggered the bloodcurdling scream from Wanda, which frightened Chloe half out of her mind, causing her to drop the mouse, who—understandably—ran for its life.

"My mouse!"

"My God, a mouse!"

"My mouse!"

"Where'd it go?"

"My God, a mouse!"

"There. There."

"Anybody home?"

"My mouse!"

"Quick. Get it."

"There."

"What's happening here?"

"I'm fine, dear. Lydia, I may have to call you back. It's . . . there. There."

"Get it, Chloe."

"Aw! There it goes!"

"My mouse! Daddy, look out."

"There. Catch it. There."

"My God, a mouse!"

Gus did a high-stepping jig when the rodent passed between her feet, then grabbed the first thing she touched off the countertop—a plastic bowl. Cautious as a lion tamer, slow as a postal worker on Valium, she trapped the cornered mouse under it.

"I got it. I got it."

"Chloe, how did I tell you to bring it over to show Gus?"

"In its cage."

"And where is its cage?"

"Who are these people?"

"At home, but I had her in my pocket and I was holding her real tight. And then she screamed," she said, pointing an accusing finger at Wanda.

"Augusta? These are friends of yours?"

"She scared my mouse," Chloe said, frowning with animosity. "It wriggled right out of my fingers."

"Hello. I'm Scott Hammond. . . ." Dimples dented, but went unnoticed as Wanda's attention was directed at the child.

"You startled me. I'm not used to having mice stuck in my face. I mean, you'd be expecting something like that from a little boy, but . . ."

"Mother, these are my next-door neighbors. My friends. My—" How to put it delicately?

". . . And this is my daughter, Chloe."

"Obviously," she said.

"I'm sorry about all this. I didn't realize you were here already. How was your trip?"

"The cabbie was a cretin, but other than that it was fine," she said, looking at him directly for the first time. "Are there any others?"

"What? Children? No, it's just me and Chloe next door."

"Oh. Oh, yes. The next-door neighbor," she said, and even though Gus hadn't mentioned him to her mother, there was a light of recognition in her eyes.

Lydia. . . .

"And your daughter," Wanda added, her appraising stare moving from Scotty to the frown on Chloe's face. Wanda started thinking so fast that Gus could actually hear the whirring of gears. "I'm very fond of little girls. I had two of my own once, but now they're all grown up. And do you know that I once saved thousands of mice from being put to death? At a pharmaceutical company. Hundreds of thousands of them, just like yours. I'm actually very fond of all animals," she said, sucking up to Chloe in the most conspicuous fashion.

Ingratiating oneself to the daughter to get to the father was such an obvious ploy—Gus blushed from the tips of her toes to the roots of her hair.

"Why don't you get . . . What did you name your mouse?"

"Annabelle," Chloe said, wary but open to a diplomatic relationship.

"Well, why don't you get Annabelle out from under that bowl and come into the living room so I can drink my tea in comfort, and I'll tell you all about saving the mice," she said, then turning her overpowering personality on Scotty, she smiled and said, "I understand you're a man with a calling. . . ."

TEN

It wouldn't be fair to say that Wanda moved in and took over Gus's life . . . it was more like she was just *there*, and really, *really* comfortable. Certainly, more comfortable than Gus was—but then, hadn't that always been the way of it with them? Wanda taking the ups and downs of Gus's life in her stride, propelling them both on to the next step, the next audition, the next accomplishment, the next performance, the next failure. . . .

"Don't you worry about a thing, sweetie," she'd said that morning. "I'll have dinner ready on the table when the three of you finish dress rehearsal. Then I'll take my Chloe girl next door, give her a bath, put her to bed, and read her a couple stories until she falls asleep. I can watch television over there as well as I can here, and you two can have a few minutes alone . . . or several hours if you want. I'm not so old I can't remember how it is to be young and in love."

Something evil in her heart wished her mother was that old. Forgetfulness could be a blessing sometimes, but aside from that she could at least look more her age, if she couldn't act it. Even after years of sun worshiping and the fifty-six years of living she'd admit to, she still looked way too young and too vibrant and too full of life.

"Mother," she said, hurrying to get dressed for school. "Please. Scotty has to leave school early to pick Chloe up, then drive all the way back in time for dress rehearsal. He'll be too tired to do anything after dinner, number one. And number two, you don't need to keep toadying up to him. He likes you. So does Chloe." Was that galling, or what? She turned her back and, lifting her hair, waited for a zip. "And three, don't you think that would be a little obvious?"

Wanda zipped. "Don't be silly, number one. Number two, I don't toad, I owe him a favor. And three, no more so than the two of you."

Gus had to take the time to mentally line up the answers and came up with, "What favor?"

"Delivering all my rain forest pamphlets," she said, going back to her coffee and the morning paper. "He said he knew all the best places in town to take them for the best distribution."

"Mother. You didn't. Not now. Not when he has so many other things on his mind. Chloe. The play. The high school. The house. The . . ."

Wanda looked up with a frown. "I know what that

boy has on his mind and believe me, delivering a few hundred pamphlets isn't going to cool it any."

Gus tsked. "Mother."

Wanda tsked. "Augusta."

"I'm serious."

"So am I. So is he, for that matter. I've never seen a man more in love with someone than he is with you."

"You think?" she asked after a brief hesitation.

"I know."

She sighed and left the room, wishing she had a fraction of her mother's confidence. Wishing she knew if a powerful love could defeat shame and disillusionment. Wishing the test of their love would come before *she* ended up on drug therapy. . . .

"All the DRUG FREE SCHOOL ZONE signs will have to come down now," Carrie Mutrux said, slipping into her train of thought as she fell into the seat beside her. "These kids are on something. Look at them. The Munchkins look as if they're sitting on anthills. Dorothy can't remember half her lines. The Tin Man keeps falling over his own feet, and the Lion isn't a coward, he's an idiot. He hasn't caught a cue yet."

"And yesterday we ran through the whole thing without a hitch. Maybe they are on drugs . . . or maybe they'd look better if we were on drugs." The two of them laughed and shook their heads. "Let's just hope that what they say about horrible dress rehearsals is true and tomorrow night will be perfect."

Scotty and his three assistant directors were milling about in the crowd onstage, talking to this one, reminding another to do this or that, rearranging props, shouting out lighting orders.

"At this point anything would be an improvement," Carrie said, curling a finger at a Munchkin who belonged to her personally. The rest were sitting—squirming and bobbing really—in the first eight rows of seats to the left of the stage in front of them. "What's the matter with everyone tonight?" she asked her solemn little first-grader—a miniature of his older brother Stevie—straightening the pink and yellow daisy hat perched on his head. "Are you tired of sitting? Getting hungry? I think we're almost finished, if you could just sit still a little—"

"I am sittin' still, Mom," he said, looking back at his classmates.

"Honey, you were moving from seat to seat. I saw you."

"That girl's gonna hurl, Mom. She'll get my costume dirty. And I don't want to get it on me anyhow."

"What? What girl?"

"Chloe. Ms. Miller's friend from the other school. She's all red in the face, and she says she's thinkin' 'bout getting sick."

Frowning at each other, the two women were on their feet and heading for the middle of Munchkin Land. In seconds they spotted Chloe drooping over the arm of her seat like a limp begonia, the seats around her having been cautiously cleared. Her face was indeed flushed almost as red as her hat, and her eyes were closed.

"Chloe?" Gus said, making her way through

short, busy legs to get to her. "Chloe, honey? Are you sick?"

Brown eyes looked at her, dazed, glassy, and watery. Without a doubt it was the most pathetic thing Gus had ever seen. Her heart twisted painfully in her chest as she sat down beside her and wrapped her arms around the listless child.

"Baby, you're burning up. Why didn't you say something?"

"I want to be in the play."

"I know, sweetie. But not if you're sick. Come on. Come with me, Chloe. We'll tell your daddy, and then one of us will take you home."

"But I want to stay in the play. Will I be better tomorrow?"

"I don't know. We'll have to wait and see. Come on now. Aw, you just don't feel good at all, do you?"

Hanging her head, she shook it no and followed Gus into the aisle. Carrie, knowing a sick child when she saw one, had gone to fetch Scotty, who was coming at them with long, purposeful strides.

"What's this? We have a sick Munchkin, do we?" he said, a sympathetic smile on his face as he went down on one knee beside his daughter. Putting his hand on the most obvious symptom, he asked softly, "Can you tell me what's wrong, Chlo?"

Again she shook her head and let her face fall into the curve of his neck. Automatically he picked her up and held her in his arms, rocking gently back and forth.

"I'll take her home," he said, casting a quick

glance over the entire proceedings, running down his mental list to be sure everything else he was responsible for was being taken care of.

"Or I can," Gus said, worried and wanting to stay with them. "Or maybe she should go to a hospital. She's so hot and she looks so . . . Actually, I can handle everything here for you, so you take her to the hospital and I'll come as soon as I can."

"No, no. I'll take her home for now. But I'd appreciate it if you'd hang around here and keep an eye on my directors. They know what's going on and what's needed, if you'll just help them out."

"Yes, of course. Go. Call Mother over if you need her, she's good in a crisis. And call me . . . well, no . . . I'll be home as soon as I can. Don't worry about anything here. Dress rehearsals are always terrible. Everything will be fine. Chloe's what's important now and she—"

To everyone's amazed delight, he leaned over and silenced her babble with a quick kiss on the lips.

"She'll be fine," he said, as much for his sake and Chloe's as for hers. "Kids get suddenly sick and suddenly better all the time. *You* call me if you have any trouble, and I'll see you later."

"Okay," she said, watching them walk away. Chloe opened her eyes to look back and flap an arm good-bye, and Gus blew her a kiss. She stood there even when they were gone from sight, worried and wondering and realizing that he'd just left with two huge chunks of her heart—and if she wanted to continue to live, she needed to be with them, close to them, remain connected with them somehow.

"Come on," Carrie said, draping an understanding arm across her shoulders. "The sooner we get this comedy of errors whipped into shape, the sooner we can go home."

"Do you think she'll be all right? I know next to nothing about children. I feel so . . ."

"Helpless?" she asked, turning her back toward the stage. "Well, welcome to motherhood, Ms. Miller. You may as well get used to that feeling. When they're little you can fix every toy they own with superglue, heal their wounds with a bandage and a kiss. You're their hero. But the older they get, the more helpless you become. And not just when they're sick. When you can't mend friendships for them or protect them from cruel words or from failure and disappointment, that's when you feel helpless. Chloe will be fine. You make her some gelatin, give her a hug, and read her stories till she feels better . . . that's easy. But there won't be much you can do about the unhappiness she'll feel when she realizes she won't be in the play tomorrow night. That's when you feel helpless. When there's nothing you can do to fix it, and no way to make her feel better inside," she said, thumping her chest lightly with her fist. "That's when you're truly helpless, and it can be very painful."

With those wise and not so reassuring words, she dashed off to break up a bickerment in the Emerald City.

Gus sighed and began to think of all the ramifications her idea of involving Chloe as a Munchkin was having on the people she loved. It was all her fault. Granted, it was an innocent suggestion, but if she'd kept her big mouth shut, none of this would be happening. Chloe would still be with her mother and maybe she wouldn't have gotten sick at all and . . . Oh! Chloe's mother had gone off for a romantic Thanksgiving vacation with her boyfriend thinking Chloe would be just fine, being in the play and celebrating the holiday with her father afterward. But what if Chloe was seriously ill? Could she be reached in time? Or . . . or what if it was something minor, but enough to keep her out of the play? Would their sympathy be enough to console her sadness? Would she for an instant believe she'd failed or disappointed her father, or Gus, if she couldn't participate? It was important that she know her illness couldn't have been prevented, that the suggestion had been made with her happiness in mind, that any pleasure Gus received from it was in seeing her happy—that any sorrow she might see in the faces of those who loved her was simply a reflection of what they were seeing in her. It was empathy, an understanding, an attempt to share in her unhappiness.

Scotty had been so excited for her, so pleased to be able to involve her in his life—it would be supremely important that he let her know his disappointment was *for* her, not *in* her. Chloe was always so eager to please him, to impress him.

She remembered the disappointment in her mother's eyes, time after time, failure after failure.

Her heart twisted in pure misery at the thought of Chloe seeing it in Scotty's face.

All the way home she thought about it. Being helpless. Being tossed about by fate, in spite of all the efforts you'd taken to control your own destiny. What was the point? Why bother? What difference did it make? she wondered. It was as futile as trying to catch the moon in a bushel basket or building sand castles at low tide.

Failure after failure, and she'd gotten back up, dusted herself off, and gone after the next best dream—only to fail again and again. All that work. All that pain. And for what? To have providence slap her down, kick her into a corner, leave her wounded and bleeding, to die in Tylerville?

Crazy thing was, she didn't really feel wasted. She thought about Scotty and Chloe and the children at school. With no effort at all she relived the contentment she felt playing the music she wanted to play, when she wanted to play it—just for the love of it. The rare moments when she saw the awe and wonder in a pupil's face when they discovered they could make their violin sing, when an accidental movement was right on and then became something purposeful. She smiled. Once again she had one of those overwhelming sensations of knowing she was happy.

Sooo . . . maybe fate wasn't such a bad thing. Maybe her destiny had been in Tylerville all along. Maybe providence knew her better than she knew herself.

And what about her free will? What about the

dreams she'd had, the efforts she'd made, the few great accomplishments she had attained? They weren't a waste either, she realized. It was interesting to think of all the things she'd learned from her various teachers. Chilling to recall the sense of being special and unique as a child, without being so gifted as to make her feel like a freak of nature. Maybe there was some sort of mystic balance between one's free will and one's destiny. Maybe true greatness was achieved only by those Fate believed could handle it well—or by those who couldn't handle it but needed to know that for an entirely different purpose in life.

Perhaps, just perhaps, she'd reached the pinnacle of her talent at a young age with the certain knowledge that she'd never achieve more. And then lost it all, because she was meant to do something else—yet would never have been happy at it if she hadn't gone as far as she could in the other direction?

Yes, maybe Tylerville and Scotty and Chloe had been her destiny all along—but she wouldn't have known how happy she was if she didn't know how *un*happy she'd been somewhere else. . . .

"How is she?" she asked, having gone directly to Scotty's house, knocking and calling out her entrance. He'd called her up to Chloe's room. "Did you call the doctor? Is her fever down?"

She was leaning over the little girl, caressing her cheek with the backs of her fingers before he could get two words out.

"I gave her some Tylenol and your mother was

over here for a while. She says you've had chicken pox."

"Chicken pox?"

He nodded. "In the time it took me to get ahold of Janis and find out she'd been exposed, your mother was up here putting calamine lotion on the spots all over her body. She says there'll be more tomorrow."

"Aw, poor baby," she said, watching Chloe's eyes flutter open. "How are you doing?"

"Your hand feels good," she murmured. She was lethargic and flushed still, and looked to be totally miserable.

"Nice and cool from outside, huh?" She used the hand she hadn't heated up on the child's face to cool her brow. "You know what I'm going to do? I'm going home to change my clothes and then I'm coming back here to do something very special to you, that my mommy used to do to me when I was sick. Would you like that?"

She shrugged, too sick to care one way or another. But since it was one of the fonder memories she had of her own mother, Gus decided she'd definitely come back and bathe her face with cool rose water and a supersoft cloth.

"Is her mother coming?" she asked in a whispered voice when her eyes slowly closed again. "This must be awful for her."

He smiled and gave a soft laugh. "Not really. In fact, I think she's sort of relieved," he said, hanging an arm across her shoulder and leading her out of the room. "She apologized for letting her come here after being exposed, but the incubation period from the first exposure was up two days ago, and Chloe was fine then. She assumed they'd missed her this time. And she did offer to come home and take care of her, but I told her I thought I could handle a childhood disease—that maybe it was my turn. So we agreed that she'd stay where she was for now and we'd see how things went. And Chloe doesn't seem to be upset that she isn't here, so maybe we won't need her this time."

"How can the two of you be so calm about this?"

"We've been through it before. Not the chicken pox, but ear infections when she was little, and the flu and colds. Kids are tougher than they look. And as long as you know what's wrong with them, it's not so bad."

"It's terrible. She looks so weak and lifeless. I hate seeing her like this. I'd rather have her bouncing off the walls than laying there like that."

He chuckled. "Wait till her fever breaks. We'll have to sit on her to keep her in bed and tie her hands to the bedposts to keep her from scratching. By the time she's finished with the chicken pox, you won't think she's so weak and lifeless."

This remained to be seen, but there were other complications here as well. "Has she said anything about missing the play?"

"She thinks she'll be better by tomorrow. Want some coffee?" he asked heading down the stairs.

"Well, when she's not better by tomorrow, you'll have to be careful not to let her see how disappointed you are that she can't be in the play."

"Why?" he asked, not bothering to look back at her as she followed him into the kitchen. "I mean, why would she think I'd be any more disappointed than she is? I only allowed her to be in the play to make her happy. I won't be disappointed if she's not."

"I know that. And you know that. But will she?"

"Sure. Why wouldn't she? Would you rather have tea?"

He just wasn't getting it.

"No. Maybe when I get back." She hesitated to go further. "I just think we should be careful that she doesn't misconstrue our sympathy for her as some sort of disappointment in her for getting sick and missing the play, is all."

"She won't," he said, almost absently as he poured himself a cup of coffee. Then he went stone-still, and after a second or two he turned to her.

There was a strange look in his eyes. One she'd not seen before. A cold, no-nonsense, almost ruthless sort of warning. Something instinctive and primitive prickled the small hairs on the back of her neck.

"I think I see where you're going with this," he said, his tone level enough, but as cool as the expression on his face. "And I don't want you filling Chloe's head with notions of failure and disappointment. Those words aren't part of her vocabulary yet. Feeling like a failure and thinking you've disappointed everyone you've ever cared about is your problem, not hers."

Each razor-sharp word slashed at her heart. Tears

stung at the back of her eyes. Her throat felt thick and stiff as she swallowed and tried to deny his accusation.

"I . . ." She looked away, then back again. "I didn't mean . . ."

"I know." A small lopsided smile worked at his lips and understanding warmed his eyes. "I know you'd never hurt her intentionally." He closed the distance between them. Rubbed her upper arms in a consoling, regretful manner. "But I see how easy it's been for you to blame yourself for everything that's ever gone wrong around you, and . . . I don't want that for my daughter. I don't want it for you."

A huge "but" hung in the air between them, insinuating that it was too late for her, that there was nothing he could do to change her thinking, *but* he still had some control over Chloe's life.

There didn't seem to be anything she could say. He was aware of what she'd been trying to tell him, and Chloe *was* his daughter. He hadn't said it straight out, but "butt out" was the message she received.

And Scotty saw the delivery. In her inability to look at him, the lowering of her eyes to withdraw herself. And all she'd been trying to do was warn him to be careful.

"Be sure to thank your mother for dinner, will you?" he said, lifting her face to his with one finger under her chin, a plea for forgiveness gentling his voice. She searched his eyes and found nothing but tender understanding and love in them. It was over. He was as sorry now as he'd been protective of his child moments earlier. "She brought me some earlier.

Sorry, I didn't wait for you, but she said it would get cold if I did, and I was starving—"

"No," she said quickly, glad for a change of subject, eager to give up on her unsolicited parenting lessons—wanting to hide her bruised emotions. "I'm glad you ate. We could have been at rehearsal all night, for all you knew."

"Lord, I forgot all about it," he said with a laugh. "Get everything ironed out?"

"We tried, but it was still a pretty lumpy mess when the parents started showing up for their kids."

She took a few minutes more to fill him in on the possible disasters facing them the next evening and then went home. To change clothes, to eat, and to borrow rose water from her mother, who was brimming over with reminiscences of chicken pox long gone.

"What do you think, Chloe? You like that?" she asked a short while later, tenderly dabbing the little face here and there with a cool, damp cloth. Her temperature had taken an upward swing again while she was gone and Scotty had repeated the medicine to bring it back down. He'd gone downstairs to make some phone calls when she got back. "I can stop if you don't like it."

She shook her head on the pillow. "It smells good."

"It does, doesn't it. That's roses. Maybe next summer you and I can plant some in my garden and smell them all summer long. Would you like that?"

She nodded. The despondency was killing Gus.

She didn't know if the little girl was depressed or if she simply didn't have the energy to talk.

"You know, Chloe, there's a chance that you might not be well enough to be in the play tomorrow night," she said gently, thinking twice before she broached the subject but needing with all her heart to be sure Scotty was right. "If you're not, I want you to know that no one blames you for getting sick. It's not your fault. In fact, we're all very unhappy that it had to happen to you."

"I know," she said blandly. "Stuff happens sometimes."

"That's right, it does," she said, extremely impressed with the child's wisdom. "And most of the time there's nothing you can do to stop it. It just happens. But it never changes the way people feel about you."

"I know. Will you make it cold again, Gus?"

Quickly dipping the cloth back in the cool water and wringing it out, she went back to pressing it against her face.

"Your daddy and your mommy love you very, very much. And so do I."

"No matter what," she said, and it wasn't a question.

"That's right," Gus said, her eyes blurring with tears. "No matter what."

She couldn't help the green frothy envy that bubbled over inside her. Not thick and resentful, who could feel that for a child? But a certain longing for the confidence Chloe felt in the love around her, the unquestioning faith in it. Was it something all children had? Something some of them lost in adulthood? Or something special between certain parents and their offspring?

"My mommy and daddy got divorced," she said, her eyes closed, her voice low and tired sounding. "For no good reason. For nobody's fault. It just happened. But we still love each other. No matter what."

"That's right," Gus said, after a moment of realization. It was taught, this love Chloe knew. Carefully nurtured. Protected by her parents. The confidence and faith came naturally, because it had never let her down, never failed her.

She closed her eyes on the stinging urge to cry again. Her mother loved her. So had her father in his own way. She'd always known that, so what had happened? Had her failures been too great? Her brain grew hot and started to fry as she tried to remember one time her mother had expressed resentment or dissatisfaction or . . . any real negative emotion toward her, and couldn't. It had never been anything more than a brief sadness in her eyes. And then she'd bustled around and hustled them off to the next audition, the next teacher, the next competition.

"Gus . . ." Chloe muttered plaintively. Glancing down at the cloth in her hands, she quickly wrung it out again and went back to cooling her off.

"You're a very lucky little girl, Chloe."

Several seconds went by, then Chloe sighed and murmured, "Mostly I am, but not with chicken pox."

Her mother had red lipstick dots all over her face and arms.

"Chloe and I have been suffering together all day," she was saying, the next evening. She pushed a few stray strands of blond- and gray-streaked brown hair out of her face as she cut the sandwich she was making Gus in half. "She was a little worried about all the spots, but after I got mine, she hasn't given them a second thought."

"Are you, ah, planning to go around looking like that until all Chloe's spots are gone?" she asked, sitting at the kitchen table, watching her ladle soup out of a pot.

"Good grief no. She's over the initial shock and her fever broke this afternoon. She'll be able to cope with it all much better tomorrow. *Then*, after that, the itching starts. And I've never seen so many spots on one child. We're going to have a terrible time with that." Gus smiled at the way she automatically included herself. "I promised her that once all the spots scabbed over, we'd play connect the dots with a Magic Marker."

"You always were fun in a crisis, Mother."

"And you were always such a stick in the mud," she said, laughing, giving her a quick hug as she set the soup and sandwich in front of her. "Always so serious."

"It was nice of you to stay with her, so Scotty could go to work today," she said, feeling a little awk-

ward. She'd been thinking about her mother all day—
and she was beginning to see that she might not know
her as well as she thought she did. "And missing the
play tonight, to stay home with her. Eric'll be sorry
you're not there."

"Eric won't notice if I'm there or not, he'll be so
nervous and excited. And I'll see him tomorrow night,
at the grand finale. What?" she asked, catching Gus
watching her. "No. Don't tell me. You're thinking I
look like an idiot with all these spots, but I don't
care. I—"

"Actually, I was remembering when you did that
for me and Liddy when we had chicken pox."

"Did I look this stupid then?"

She nodded solemnly, studying her mother as if
she'd never seen her before.

"Oh, sweetie, don't be mad at me. I swear it'll
come right off with a little cold cream and some elbow grease. I'd have used washable markers if you had
any, or ketchup if I thought it would have stayed on.
Honestly, they don't use the same kinds of dyes in
cosmetics that they used to. I won't have spots for
days and days the way I did last time and—"

"Mother. I'm not mad. I like your spots."

"You do?"

Again she nodded. "I've been thinking
lately . . ."

"Oh no," she said, setting her own supper on the
table and slumping into the chair across from her.
"Not again."

"What?"

"Every time you say you've been thinking and get that look on your face, I know it's trouble. I thought you were happy here."

"I am happy here. Will you let me talk? You never let me talk."

"You usually don't want to," she said, then added, "but go ahead. I'm listening."

"I've been thinking lately," she repeated with emphasis, "that I probably don't tell you often enough or show you often enough, that I really do love you and . . ."

"Well, I love you, too, sweetheart. I . . ."

"Mother."

"Sorry."

"I'd also like to apologize for all the times I've failed you. I know how much time and energy you dedicated to me and to my career, and I don't think I ever said thank you. I . . . wish I could have been all the things you were hoping I'd be, part of me wishes things had turned out differently, but they didn't and . . . and I'm sort of glad they didn't, but I know I disappointed you and I'm sorry for that."

Wanda sat staring at her with a frown on her face, glancing away briefly, then back at her in confusion.

"Honey, I don't know what you're talking about." She hesitated. "You're right, about us not saying and showing our love very often, but sometimes it's like that in families. People are together so long, know each other so well, that those feelings are simply assumed. It doesn't mean . . ."

"Well, they shouldn't be. Assumed. You should

know for sure that I love you, and you should know that Eric *will* miss you tonight."

Wanda looked embarrassed and smiled a little. Slowly she said, "I am glad to know those things. And just for the record, you should know that I love you too."

"I do. But I don't think I realized how much until just recently."

Her smile grew a little wider and she gave a soft laugh, her eyes going misty with memories.

"I used to wonder where you and Lydia came from, you were both so different and neither of you had anything in common with me." She laughed softly and took a spoonful of soup. "Not even clothes. You always wore dresses and Lydia liked her pressed slacks and button-down collars. And there I was in jeans and gauze blouses, my hair a different color every six months, my earrings hanging down to my boobs . . . people were always so surprised when they saw us together." She looked directly at Gus. "And I was in a constant state of awe. There was Liddy, so organized and competent and down-to-earth. And you," she shook her head, "so gifted and bright and such a perfectionist. Not shy and withdrawn and looking for a quiet life like your father, or loud and brassy and looking to change the world like me. Neither one of us could figure out how the two of you came from the two of us."

"And he was so disappointed he had to leave."

Wanda looked disturbed. "That's twice you've used that word, disappointed. I told you, he was looking for a quiet life, Augusta. He left because he knew he'd never have one with me. I used to drive him crazy." She laughed. "Running off to riot here or protest there. If it was local, I'd take the two of you with me, but usually it was too far away, so I'd leave you with him and be gone for weeks. He was constantly bailing me out of jail. It was the sixties. Well, the seventies, too, pretty much. He just got fed up with it, honey. But he was never disappointed in anyone. Not even me. He used to say he was proud of my work, of the way I felt about things. It just wasn't the sort of life he wanted. So he left."

"Did he know . . . about me?" She turned her left hand over on the table. "About the operation?"

"I don't know. I lost track of him years ago. And that's sad. Something I regret, because I know he would have been very proud of you. As proud as I am."

Am? Still?

Gus shook her head and sailed her spoon back and forth in her soup. "I would have let him down too."

"I don't see how," she said, spooning more soup into her mouth, then picking up her sandwich. "You were already playing the violin better than he could when he left. And I know for a fact that it pleased him very much."

Once again, they were talking around the subject of her failure. Life before and life since but not about the actual failure.

"Mother," she said, leaving the spoon in the bowl to fist both hands on the table in front of her. "I failed. I blew it. All your work. All the scholarships you got me, the tryouts and the teachers, all the running around, the move to New York, the time, the money, your hopes and dreams . . . I wasted all of it. I let you down. I failed you." She blinked back tears. As painful as it was to say, it was also a relief to have it out in the open, to have it said. "I'm sorry for that. For disappointing you. I really am."

Wanda set her sandwich aside as she shook her head in confusion and denial.

"Never," she said, emphatically. "Not once in all your life have you ever been a disappointment to me, young lady. If anything, you've been an inspiration." Now it was Gus's turn to look confused. "Sweetheart, I didn't get you those scholarships, you earned them. The most I ever did *for* you was to put you in opportunity's path. You did the rest. You're the one who practiced for hours on end until the music was perfect. You're the one who impressed the teachers and the conductors. Not me. You were the one who played that violin so beautifully, and whose heart was broken whenever things went wrong. Not me. All I could do was stand by helplessly and watch."

"Helplessly?" There was that word again. She knew what it was to feel helpless when someone she loved was hurting. Carrie Mutrux knew about it too. So did Scotty.

Wanda picked up her soup spoon again. "There's nothing worse, believe me, than feeling and knowing you're helpless to help someone you love," she said, matter of fact. "I'd watch your dream come tumbling down and feel so miserable for you. But it was always much harder on you, because you were always so hard on yourself." Then her face brightened. "Then suddenly one day you'd say, 'Mother, I've been thinking,' and you'd be off on another dream. Your resilience has always astounded me. I've never known anyone as strong or as determined as you. Even this last time, after the surgery," she said, glancing over at Gus with watery eyes. "Afterward, when I knew you'd never play the same way and you kept practicing . . . I thought it was going to kill me, watching you. Working so hard. Your hopes so high . . ." She blinked the tears away. "And now look at you. A whole new life. You seem happier and more content than I've ever seen you before. I . . . I'm so proud of you."

Gus's gaze slowly lowered to the table and then to the food in front of her. In her mind, newfound puzzle pieces were falling into place, falling from the sky to fit neatly into the picture of a mother simply loving her child.

"You never felt cheated?" she asked mildly. "Of your time? All the sacrifices you made?"

"Sure I did," she said. "Moving to New York was damned inconvenient. And I hated having you away at school all those years. And I had to learn all about being a professional violinist—the right way to go, who to see, what to do—which I don't mind telling you I had no interest in at all. And at concerts and recitals, listening to fifty other young violinists when I only came to hear you—that was a damned drag." She took a mouthful of soup and swallowed. "But when you have children you do these things. For them. Because you love them. And you never regret it. You'll see when you have your own children, Augusta." She looked up at the kitchen clock. "Which reminds me, I'd better hurry and finish here, Scotty will be wanting to leave for the play soon. And I haven't cut out the finger gelatin molds for Chloe yet. And you . . ."

"Mother?"

"Yes?"

"I love you."

"Of course you do. Now hurry or you'll be late too."

ELEVEN

"Okay, now I'm really getting worried," Scotty said, his voice loud in the silence they'd been cruising along in on their way to the school. He glanced at her, then back at the road. "You're being awfully quiet over there. You're not worried about your Munchkins, are you? Because even if they forget all the words to the songs, their costumes are cute enough to get a standing ovation. It's more fun when the little kids screw up anyway. Gives the parents something to talk about for the rest of their lives," he said, rattling on in the darkness. "I was a tree in the second grade, and my parents razzed me about rubbing my nose and scratching my backside until the day they died. And they all have camcorders now, so they can get it all on tape. Emotional blackmail. Parents live for that sort of stuff." A very brief pause. " 'Course, it's only cute when they're little. Kids expect more of themselves when they get older. Not screwing up becomes a matter of pride and—"

"Who's worried here? You or me?"

He looked at her. "Me," he said honestly. "I'm wondering now if maybe we shouldn't have waited until after Christmas to do this. Maybe I rushed it. A few more weeks of rehearsal wouldn't have hurt. Some of the juniors and seniors have been studying for the SATs during all this—"

"Scotty."

Again he glanced her way.

"My Munchkins could do this in their sleep, and your kids are having the time of their life. If we'd waited till after Christmas vacation, we would have lost the momentum, it would have gotten old and they'd have been bored. They're ready now. And if they flub up tonight, they'll cover it up and talk about it at class reunions fifty years from now." His gaze met hers and she smiled. "You can't make everything perfect for them all the time. You can't always wait for the right time and the right circumstances and the right position of the stars. If the opportunity presents itself, you lead them to it and then it's up to them. You wanted it to be a learning experience. Success and failure are things they need to learn about too."

"They'll have the rest of their lives to learn those lessons. They don't need me to—"

"But they won't have the rest of their lives to learn how to handle it," she said, cutting him off. "They won't always have the support system they have now, with each other and with us. They're going to be fine tonight. But even if they do make a few mistakes, they need to know that life goes on, that they're going to make plenty of mistakes before they're finished, and life will still go on."

He cast her a considering look.

"So, snap out of it," she said, and she laughed. "They're looking to you for their confidence. And you look about as sure as a dentist with an instruction manual under his arm."

He let loose a tight chuckle and sighed. She could see him mentally ordering his body to relax, his shoulders to straighten up, his worried frown to dissipate. Then his eyes narrowed, and he slipped another look at her.

"This isn't your usual doom and gloom lecture. You're the one who sees disaster around every corner, not me. Am I . . . would I happen to be . . ." he did a cocky little swagger with his head, ". . . rubbing off on you? Getting under your skin? Changing your perspective on life?"

"Humph," she snorted.

"Well then," he said, his tone of voice thankful and full of affection. "Tell me when you got to be so smart."

"I've always been smart," she said. *I just didn't know it*, she thought.

Alissa Dumark of the Lullaby League was extremely excited and more than a little hammy, dancing alone well after the chorus started singing again.

The Lollipop Guild and their striped tights were a huge hit. The children sang loud and a little off key. And Dorothy didn't trip over a single Munchkin on her way out of town. . . . So, all in all, Gus's part of the play was a great success.

She and Carrie herded the children into the library to wait for the final scene. With a sigh of relief, she then turned her nail-biting to the rest of the play.

Backstage she helped with whatever she could, so pleased that whenever the Tin Man tripped over his feet he somehow made it look as if it were purposeful. The audience loved it. And when the stuffed Toto fell out of Dorothy's basket, she ad-libbed a reprimand for him to stay put. Lisa Witt, who played the Wicked Witch of the West, had the most god-awful piercing cackle that night, it was blood-chilling. And Heather Preston didn't teeter once as she sailed across the stage as Glinda, the Good Witch of the North.

Gus stood among the curtains stage right and watched them. The student actors, their families in the audience, their pals helping out backstage. Scotty smiled at her once from stage left but was too busy to see the impact the evening was having on her.

It was as if, after years of eating away at the earth's crust—at her crust of self-doubt and fear—a new geyser had suddenly broken through, erupted inside her. Shooting forth a hot stream of understanding and with it some confidence and contentment, the steam filling the air around it with love and happiness and hope.

In a moment of intense peace, she saw herself in a

thousand pictures that flashed through her mind. She knew who she was, who she had been, where she was, where she had been. She found a pristine pride in herself, something she'd never known before. She stroked it tenderly, fed it with memories long forgotten.

She felt free and giddy inside. And just as Dorothy was about to discover the true identity of the Wizard, Gus was discovering that she wasn't some extraordinary creature with the power to crush other people's hopes and dreams and expectations.

She was just a simple woman who could play a violin really, really well, who was head over heels in love with a man and his little girl—with only enough power to make herself happy.

Dashing back to the library to lead the Munchkins back for the finale, she knew exactly what spectacular feat she wanted to accomplish next in her life, and just exactly how to go about it.

"Oh! Auntie Em, there's no place like home," Dorothy cried out dramatically.

The floor vibrated and the rafters shook with applause. The curtains closed and opened on the citizens of the Emerald City, and the Munchkins bowed. Each character in turn took a bow.

And then the students and the audience began to clamor around Scotty.

Watching from backstage, her heart felt as if it were splitting at the seams with love and pride as she watched him. He exuded a perfect mix of humility and confidence as he walked out onstage with his students.

He might not be King Midas, she thought, knowing now that the mystery of his powers had more to do with hard work and determination than magic, but there was definitely something about him that made her heart feel golden.

A true master of manipulation, he took less credit than he gave, citing the students' hard work and the selfless contributions made by members of the community—endearing him to the masses and stoking enthusiasm for next year's project. When he finally got to the subject of Carrie Mutrux's invaluable help and her own efforts with the Munchkins, he wasn't happy to let them merely wave from one side of the stage, but motioned them over closer to him, center stage.

Smiling, she automatically took his outstretched hand in hers and waved at the crowd once more. He asked the ladies of the Garden Club to stand in appreciation of their work on the Kansas costumes, and while they were doing their own waving, she caught his eye and smiled at him.

"What?" he asked, the look in her eyes shaking something deep inside him, making him a little nervous. "What? What's going on?"

"Nothing," she said innocently, with a wily smirk.

He frowned at her, then announced the contributions of several local businessmen and women.

He cast her a suspicious glance during their applause and she said, "I was just wondering what you'll do if I give you more daughters, instead of sons?" He gave her a startled look. "What if we have twelve children together and none of them are boys?"

He dragged his gaze from hers and gave a halting introduction to the parents who helped build the scenery.

"You're talking about Plan B, right?" he asked as if they'd discussed Plans A–Z in depth. "The All Girl Kazoo Band that we take on the road?"

She laughed, and he called for the members of the Ladies Auxiliary to stand up and take credit for the lead characters' Oz costumes.

"You still want to marry me, right?" she asked him, not even looking at him, her voice hidden under the thunder of applause.

"Absolutely," he said, smiling out at the crowd. He called out a general thanks to all the parents and friends who had attended the play that night and during the final round of applause, added, "Right away."

"Good," she said, nodding her answer.

He turned to her then and, taking her by the shoulders, he kissed her. Right there in front of neighbors and friends and students and Munchkins and God and . . . everybody.

A whole new round of clapping rose up from the crowd, and they were laughing when they came apart. She looked into his eyes and, for the first time ever, saw a true reflection of herself. Her strengths and weaknesses, her joys and fears. She saw that she was capable of great things and huge mistakes at the same time, saw the rightness in that, the way it balanced her life—with the good always outweighing the bad.

Students and friends were closing in around them. She reached up and palmed his face to keep his attention just one second longer.

"You won't be disappointed, you know."

He smiled, slow and knowing, then said, "I never thought I would be."

THE EDITORS' CORNER

Think about it. How would you react if love suddenly came up and bit you? Would you be ready to accept it into your life? Well, in the four LOVE-SWEPTs we have in store for you this month, each hero and heroine has to face those questions. Love takes them by surprise, and these characters, in true-to-life form, all deal with it in different fashions. We hope you enjoy reading how they handle that thing called love!

The ever-popular Fayrene Preston continues her Damaron Mark series with **THE DAMARON MARK: THE MAGIC MAN,** LOVESWEPT #878. Wyatt Damaron is sure he's dreaming. Even so, he can't resist following the lovely woman in period dress beckoning to him from the mist. As the mist recedes, Wyatt realizes that his sweet-talking sprite is flesh-and-blood contemporary Annie Logan. Wyatt is most definitely a man unlike any Annie has been used to, but something about the danger and passion lurking in his eyes has her thinking more than twice about him. He is a spellbinding sorcerer who promises to dazzle and amaze her, and in that he doesn't fail. He'd vowed to protect Annie from all that threatens to keep them apart, but will Annie trust him long enough to let him succeed? Fayrene doesn't disappoint in this sizzling novel that powerfully explores the fate of kindred spirits whose destinies are forever entwined.

Cheryln Biggs takes you on a high-speed chase through Louisiana low country in **HIDDEN TREASURE, LOVESWEPT #879.** Slade Morgan and Chelsea Reynolds are both out to recover a priceless pair of stolen antique perfume bottles—but for different reasons. For Slade it's a job he's been hired to do, for Chelsea it's a chance to prove she can accomplish more for her company in the field than behind a desk. A dangerous game of cat and mouse ensues, making for close quarters and breathless adventure. You'll be glad you came along for the ride as one reckless rebel of a hero meets his match in an unlikely damsel in distress.

Author Catherine Mulvany returns at her humorous best with her second LOVESWEPT, #880. Mallory Scott has always had trouble trusting men. Wouldn't you be **MAN SHY** if your boyfriend of eleven years left you for your own sister? Now Mallory has to find a date for the happy couple's upcoming nuptials. But he can't be just any man, he has to be one hunk of a guy. Enter Brody Hunter. Sexy mouth, silver gray eyes, tousled chocolate brown hair—in short, drop-dead gorgeous. More than enough man to ward off the pitying looks sure to be given her at the wedding. Brody can't understand why the beautiful Mallory has to hunt for an escort, but who is he to argue with good fortune? Will the potent attraction they feel be strong enough to convince Mallory to drop the carefully planned game of let's pretend? Let Catherine Mulvany show you in this outrageous romp of a romance!

Please welcome newcomer Caragh O'Brien and her stunningly sensual debut, **MASTER TOUCH,** LOVESWEPT #881. When worldly art dealer Milo Dansforth requests art restorer Therese Carroll's services, she's not sure she wants the hassle. She's quite satisfied with her quiet existence. But Milo is counting on Therese's loyalty to her father to ensure that she'll take on the job—she's the only one with the expertise to do the restoration on his priceless portrait. In a makeshift art conservatory set up in a Boston studio, Therese races the clock to finish the project and discover the secrets that lay beneath the surface of both the painting and its mysterious owner. Milo tantalizes Therese with his every touch, and suddenly the painting is not the only thing these two lovers have in common. Caragh O'Brien's talent shines bright in this tapestry of tender emotion and breath-stealing mystique. Look for more from Caragh in the near future!

Happy reading!

With warmest wishes,

Susann Brailey

Joy Abella

Susann Brailey
Senior Editor

Joy Abella
Administrative Editor